I0541192

The Perfect Kiss

A love story of the Second Coming

Dennis O'Connell

Copyright © 2016 Dennis O'Connell

All rights reserved.

ISBN:0997556404
ISBN-13:9780997556407

DEDICATION

To God for inspiring me every day and
providing me the words to write.

CONTENTS

1   Part 1   Pg #2

2   Part 2   Pg #88

3   Epilogue   Pg #205

PART 1

CHAPTER 1

EL. Wow!

That was the first impression I had when I first saw EL and I still get the same feeling every day. I was beginning my MBA program and got to my first class a little early. So being trained well in the Presbyterian Church, I took one of the seats in the back of the room and was lazily looking out the window when she walked in. She instantly won my heart.

Over the course of the semester, I tried everything I could to catch her eye. I acted smart, I acted quiet and even tried stupid once all to no avail. With the approach of finals, I knew nothing was going to happen before the Christmas break.

One of the guys in my class who I would become great friends with, did their work/study program in Admissions. Over beers one evening, I was feeling sorry for myself and shared my romantic feelings for EL. It was then that Jeff volunteered to help. He would let me know what classes EL was going to enroll in the following semester so I could continue in my love crossed pursuit.

CHAPTER 2

Three out of my five classes had EL in them that Spring semester. Four more months of no success. Statistics was a real bitch. I learned that I was not a mathematics genius having to spend countless hours in the library and with a tutor just to get the only B I had ever received in any class. The pursuit of love can be humbling.

On the upside, I found that Economics and Computer Programming were fields I unexpectedly excelled in. The part of Economics I liked most was trying to predict the future based on past events. I know this will make a lot of economists unhappy but I sometimes felt I was a weatherman trying to determine how much snow we were going to get out of a particularly bad storm.

Computers though became my love. You could create applications that changed the world or just allowed people to have fun. You could dig deeply into modeling and simulation, take the results and apply them to so many fields of study. With my heart still out on my sleeve and no response from EL, I spent most of my hours trying to merge these two passions, creating complex economic models.

Also over the Spring semester, I created three strong friends to hang out with, Jeff, Gary and Jim. We hung out together, helped each other with our studies and on more than one occasion drank a few beers together. It was Gary who got me through Statistics based upon his sheer will.

At the end of the semester, Jeff shared with me that EL was taking two summer classes so she could finish up by the following Christmas. My time was running out so I reluctantly decided to stay on campus over the summer forgoing my plans to summer at the beach. I was able to get into both classes with EL but wasn't excited about the work it would require.

CHAPTER 3

The first class was called the Summer Intern. Our nine week semester was broken into three parts where we were paired with some of the entrepreneurial startups in the city. When I got to class and saw the assignments, I realized that I had zero chance of interacting with EL. We were on different teams visiting different companies. My heart was breaking.

The second class with EL was a series of case studies similar to the model that many Universities uses. The professor had created nine teams, one for each week, to review a case study, provide a critical analysis and then present a 10 minute summation for the class with a 20 minute Question and Answer period. What was interesting was that over the course of the summer, the nine groups would each review the same case studies. As the summer progressed the 20 minute Q&A became harder and harder.

I was in two groups with EL, weeks five and nine. Week five we reviewed Apple. We were sharp, knew our presentation backwards and forwards, presented strong and literally killed the Q&A. I was never so proud of folks I worked with. Unfortunately, EL had a family emergency and missed the first five days of the week. Jill, her best friend at the school, caught her up upon her return. Another lost opportunity.

Week nine looked to be a bust also. After two days, we were still struggling to get consensus on how to present to the class. It was then that Paul, one of our team members, asked if we could do something totally different. Up to this time, every group and every presentation had been done using PowerPoint. Paul had been on a couple of weak teams throughout the summer and felt that he needed to hit a home run to get an A in the class. We listened to his strategy and were blown away by his recommendation. So we acted on it, thankfully!

In his job before coming to school, Paul's CEO was big on "The Packet". When teams presented to the CEO, they had to use The Packet formula or weren't allow to present. The Packet included two 30 second videos, social media content, a two page written summary, one flipchart page, a posting to their Fileshare and NO PowerPoint.

EL and I had shown the greatest ability to write good content over the summer so we got volunteered to create the social media content and the two page written summary. This guaranteed I would get to spend the better part of three days with her.

My breakthrough came in an unexpected fashion. It was 9:00 pm on Day 6 and EL and I were busy putting the two page summaries together when I got a paper cut. Jokingly I showed EL and she said "Let me kiss it and make it better".

I must have given her a look of indignation because she shot back "isn't that what your mother always did"? With my sheepish grin, she knew she had me. I handed over my finger and she kissed it to make it better.

All of a sudden, her eyes are rolling into the back of her head and she is passing out. I leap for her and got there just before her head hit the floor, cradling her in my arms. She was where I always wanted her to be but…

It seemed like an eternity before her eyes opened and she looked up at me. Even today, I don't know what the look meant that she had on her face but that "kiss" changed the course of both of our lives.

CHAPTER 4

One of the other students in the library saw what was happening and immediately called 911. Within a minute, campus security was on the scene followed closely by an EMT squad. They fussed over EL for what seemed like forever and were trying fiercely to get her to go to the hospital.

She was just as adamant about not going, insisting that she would be fine. It was just a matter of being too focused on her grades, not eating enough, not sleeping enough and doing all the things college students do.

She said she would be fine in her own apartment and the EMTs finally relented as long as there was going to be someone there to watch her. That is when I accidently blurted out that "didn't your roommate fly out this morning?" If looks could kill, I was dead.

Now it was back to the hospital discussion with the EMT until EL said "Tom will stay with me. He is a good friend and we have a comfortable couch." Things had just gone from was it: good to bad; bad to good; bad to worse; or am I in heaven?

With me agreeing to be guardian angel for the night, we gathered our materials and headed to her place. When we got there, she dug out a blanket for me, thanked me and apologized for the umpteenth time and headed off to bed.

The next morning, we met our group, did the presentation and absolutely knocked it out of the park! Paul, along with all of us, ended up getting the A that he so wanted.

After class, EL thanked me again for staying with her. She promised me she would make it up to me when we got back to class in late August. She made me reserve that first Friday night that we were back for dinner, her treat. And then she stepped up and gave me a kiss on the cheek.

As she was leaving, I saw her pull out her cell phone. I'm not really sure what happened the rest of the day. Does it matter!

CHAPTER 5

"Mary, this is EL. How are you doing?", she said with an excited note in her voice.

"EL, it is 2:00 am here in Sydney. I was sleeping, that is how I was doing. This had better be good!", Mary said a little groggily.

"I found him Mary. He is here."

"How do you know it is him?", she said with doubt in her voice.

"Before we start talking, we need to change to a secure line and you need to be alone. Call me back when you can even if it is 2:00 am my time."

CHAPTER 6

"EL this is Mary. I am alone and you can tell that I'm on the secure line. Give me the low down."

"So Tom was in my case study class this semester. As a matter of fact, he has been in at least one of my classes since I started the Master's program. He has tried to be friendly to me before but I never thought to give him a second chance. Funny how it is always the ones you don't expect to fall for that you fall for."

"EL, enough with the chitchat and just tell me!"

"You never did like the long story did you?"

"No EL, I want the short version", Mary said impatiently.

"OK. I'll make the story short. Our case study class required us to do projects with different groups of people throughout the semester. We got to the last case study and I was paired with Tom and two other folks. Everyone has been doing PowerPoint presentations but Paul, one of our team, needed to hit a home baseball to get an A."

"EL, that is a home run. Baseball is the game and within the game, any player when they are at bat can hit a home run."

"Whatever Mary. You knew what I meant."

"So to continue my story, Paul wanted to do something different. It included us pulling together a two page executive overview that we printed and handed out. Since Tom and I were the best writers on the team, writing and printing out the executive overview was one of our assignments."

"Yesterday evening we are in the library printing the reports and pulling everything together. Tom got a paper cut and out of habit I said 'let me kiss and make it better'". He gave me that 'I am a big boy look' so I came back with the 'isn't that what your mother used to do' response. He relented, I gave it a kiss to make it better and the next thing I know, I am waking up on the floor, wrapped in his arms and looking into his blue eyes."

"You what EL? Did you say you passed out? How is that possible? Had you been drinking or doing anything unusual?"

"Mary, you know me."

"So what happened next EL?"

"Unfortunately, one of the other students called 911 and campus security was there in two minutes followed quickly by an EMT unit."

"You didn't go to the hospital did you EL? You didn't let them examine you? Please tell me you didn't."

"I had talked them out of taking me to the hospital and into going home until Tom blurted out that my roommate had left for the semester. If looks could have killed, he would have been twelve feet under. I recovered by talking him into being my nurse for the evening. With that settled, we headed to my apartment."

"Did you sleep with him EL?"

"NO. And he was a perfect gentleman. He slept on the couch, made me breakfast and even carried all my books to class. Reminded me of 12th grade."

"Soooo. What happened next?"

"We did our presentation. Knocked it out of the infield, got a standing ovation and all of us solidified our A in the class."

"EL. You are hopeless. You knocked it out of the ballpark not the infield."

"So if it went out of the ballpark, didn't it also go out of the infield? Logic seems to dictate that if it goes out of the ballpark, it also went out of the infield. Why do they make this game so complicated? I'll bet they didn't consult with a female when they created the rules."

"Enough EL. Back to the story. I thought you were going to make this short?"

"Well I am making this short. I left out how cute he is now that I have had the time to focus on him. Did I tell you that he was in the Air Force for six years?"

"EL! EL! Can you focus for a minute please?"

"So class was over, we walked outside together, I invited him to dinner when we come back from our three week break, I gave him a kiss on the cheek and I called you. Which you weren't happy about by the way. You know you owe me an apology for yelling at me earlier."

"EL. I am sorry for yelling at you earlier. Now please sit down."

"Why do you want me to sit down?"

"BECAUSE I AM GOING TO REALLY YELL AT YOU NOW! You just let Tom walk away and you aren't going to see him for three weeks? Do you know where he is going and what he will be doing? You can't let him out of your sight until you know."

"Mary. You are right. What am I thinking? I think I got a little discombobulated last night. Between passing out and waking up in his arms, I think my brain is out in right field."

"Left field EL. Left field."

"I don't care what field it is and see you knew what I meant again."

"What are you going to do next EL?"

"I'm not sure Mary. I think I have to leave it in God's hands for the next three weeks. Plus, I'm really tired Mary. Can we talk again tomorrow at this same time? Carry both phones with you."

"I will EL. Do you want me to come over?"

"Let me think on it. I love you Mary!"

"I love you too EL."

CHAPTER 7

"Good morning Mary", EL said sounding refreshed.

"Good morning EL. Are you feeling better today?"

"I am feeling better. I think I slept for 12 hours last night. It was one of the most restful, peaceful sleeps I can remember. My head is clear and I'm ready for whatever comes today."

"What are you going to do about Tom, EL? Are you going to reach out to him?"

"I have been thinking about that and I don't think I can. I'm not sure where he lives, if he was sticking around or if he is even that interested in me. If I push too hard, it might just fall apart. When I gave him that kiss, I also gave him my phone number and told him to give me a call on that last Friday of August around noon."

"But EL, if you just let him run around, he could get hurt."

"I am aware of that and willing to take that chance. I think it is like I said yesterday, it is in our Father's hands now."

"OK. I'll listen to your thoughts. You always had the better intuition. Do you want me to come over?"

"I think if you were here when we get together, it might be too much. I'll let you know when it is time."

"In that case, let's plan on talking in a couple of days. We can do some more scheming. Same time?"

"You bet Mary. Can't wait to see you again."

CHAPTER 8

"EL, this is Mary. Have you heard from Tom? Do you know what he is doing or where he is?"

"No Mary, I haven't. I saw one of his friends last night at one of the local pubs. We got to talking and he thought Tom was going to Ocean City, Maryland for break. He said his parents used to live there and he wanted to take a trip down memory lane."

"I thanked him for his time and headed home after one drink. Last night all I could think of was walking down the beach holding his hand."

"EL, get your head on straight. You are not really falling in love with him are you? You know that will cause problems!"

EL heard exasperation in Mary's voice.

Hoping to convince Mary of her feeling, EL said "if you could have seen what I saw in that first instant when I awoke, you would be dreaming of love also. I feel so human Mary. Sometimes it is frightening."

"El, you need to focus. You need to remember the plan."

"I know Mary. Sometimes it is just hard. By the way, how are you and what's his name doing?"

"If by what's his name, you mean Andrew, we are doing just fine. Yesterday was nice so to celebrate, we went down to the beach and did some surfing. 'Bout froze my arse off."

"EL, do you want to fly over here for a week? Andrew and I would love to host you."

"I think I'm going to pass Mary. I don't want to be thousands of miles away if Tom happened to call me unexpectedly. I'm glad you are having fun with Andrew."

"Let's talk again in a couple of day."

"Sounds good EL. You know I love you! Keep your chin up."

CHAPTER 9

"Hi Mary. Only one week until I meet with Tom. I'm getting really nervous. Do you think he likes me?"

Mary could hear the nerves in her voice.

"EL. He chased you for a year. He probably figured out how to get in your classes so he could be near you. I think he likes you."

"But Mary, I mean really likes me. You know what I mean."

"I do know what you mean EL. You are going to have to use the old EL charm."

"I don't want to use the charm. I want him to like me for who I am."

"EL. He can't know who you are remember. Mums the word. Zip the mouth. Whatever way you want to say it, you can never let him know."

"Yeah."

"So how is Andrew?"

"What Andrew? We had to stop being a thing last week. He started talking about kids, buying a house, being responsible adults so I dumped him. I am leaving for London tomorrow."

"WHAT!" as EL's coffee cup met the floor spraying coffee everywhere.

"You know me EL, I can't be tied down. This is too important a time for some guy to get stuck on me. I'm thinking I can blend in nicely in London. With my Aussie accent, they will just think I'm another transplant. I'll change my hair, get a little surgery done and no one will recognize me. We are good at that."

"Oh Mary. I'm so sorry that you are having to move on. What are you going to do in London?"

"Well, I'm thinking of running a brothel. That is something I'm good at."

"Really?"

"No! Do you think I'm stupid EL? Way too much visibility. I'm going back to school again to study business. It is a great cover. No one expects much out of students."

"Mary. You already have two business degrees."

"I know. It should make the classes easy and give me more time for fun. We don't get enough of that."

"Ok Mary. Call me when you get there to let me know you arrived safely and are settled in. And wish me luck for Friday."

"EL, you don't need luck to snag Tom. You just need your charm. But good luck anyways."

CHAPTER 10

Tom was really nervous to call EL but the promise of another evening with her was all the motivation he needed to overcome his nerves.

"EL, this is Tom. I am back at school. Just wanted to make sure we are still on for tomorrow night."

"Tom, it is great to hear from you. Yes, we are still on for tomorrow night. Do you have any place you like to go? Is there any type of food you do or don't like?"

"There isn't much food I don't like, though broccoli and asparagus do fall into that category. I'm also not much of a fish eater though I have been known to eat it if it is cooked well or I am under duress." I could hear her chuckling in the background. What a doofus.

"But I continued, my two favorite local restaurants are Campetti's Pizza and the local Brew Pub downtown. My favorite chain is Texas Road House. Great food! How about you?"

"My two favorite foods are sushi and BBQ. What are your thoughts on sushi?" El asked.

"I have acquired a taste for sushi and have come to enjoy it. Over the years, what I have come to like about sushi restaurants is you order a little, you get to enjoy that dish, you order some more, get to enjoy another dish and can continue until you are full. Do you want to do sushi EL? If so, what is your favorite restaurant?"

"Sushi it is. My favorite is the Blue Moon West. It is a smaller place on the west side. It can get somewhat busy as the night progresses so how does 7:00 pm sound?"

"I think I can handle the pressure EL. Do you want me to come by and pick you up around 7:00 then?"

"That would be great Tom. Remember this is my treat for rescuing me from the EMTs and then babysitting me through the night. OK!"

"If you insist, I'll let you treat. You know I didn't do anything special other than keeping your face from kissing the floor" I said with a smile on my face.

"Don't get too cocky" she said while laughing her head off.

"I'll see you at 7:00 tomorrow EL. Goodbye."

When I hung up I realized that my heart was beating about 150 beats per minute. I had been so scared that she would have forgotten our date, that I almost didn't breath throughout the call. Also, what was with the broccoli and asparagus stuff? She must think I'm a dork.

CHAPTER 11

"Mary, I just hung up from talking with Tom. We are set to meet at 7:00 pm tomorrow for sushi. You know how much I love sushi and he likes it too. I know this is going to go great."

"EL, slow down a little. What are you talking about sushi for and who are you going to dinner with? It is really loud here and I missed the beginning of the conversation. Give me a minute to get outside."

After what seemed like an eternity, Mary finally said "Ok EL, I am where I can hear you again."

"You are such a downer. I call you with great news and you don't get it. Tom called. You know THE TOM!"

"Oh! Oh! Tom called. Tell me all about it. I didn't think he was supposed to call until tomorrow."

"Well he got back to school a day early and called to make sure we were still on for dinner. He was so cute. You could almost hear his anxiety over the phone. And then he blurted out he doesn't like broccoli or asparagus. He made me laugh though I think he was a little embarrassed."

"So you are going out for sushi. Make sure you ask if he has any food allergies. There are a lot of unknown fish allergies and we don't want him dying on you during your first date."

"What are you going to wear?" Mary asked.

"I don't know. I think my red dress is too provocative for a first date. I think he might think I am trying to get him straight to bed."

"EL, you are trying to get him straight to bed."

"I know Mary but I would be way over dressed for the Blue Moon West. How about blue jeans and one of my cute tops. Or I have some really cute shorts with a see through top over a halter. Or, or I'm just going to have to stare at my closet until I decide I need to go buy something new. What do you think?"

"EL. You always look beautiful to me. Just don't go in your birthday suit" Mary said only half seriously.

CHAPTER 12

"Mary. I'm so glad you picked up. What do I talk about tonight? What if I make a fool of myself?" El said in a panic.

"EL. This is not like you. You are miss calm, cool and collected. What has Tom done to you? Are you sure he didn't slip you some kind of love potion when you passed out?"

"Mary, I'm not sure what is going on. I feel like a teenager again and that was so long ago. I don't think I have ever felt this way before."

"EL, I can promise you that you have never acted this way before. OK, let's do some planning for tonight. What do you have in common? What do you want to talk about?"

"The only thing we have in common is school."

"So EL, why don't you ask about what he has liked at school so far? What has been his favorite class? What class did he not like? What is the one thing he learned that he will carry with him for the rest of his life? How are those questions?"

"Mary. You are the best! I don't know what I would do without you. I could also get him to talk to me about his friends, what he likes to do and about where he came from."

"EL. Be careful on that last one. He is going to want to learn about where you came from also. What story are you going to tell him? Remember that he can go on the internet to find out historical facts so make sure you stick to the story!"

"You are such a downer Mary. Just when I was getting into this whole dating thing, you bring up our past. What if I mess up?"

"You are going to be fine EL. How many times have you told this story in the past? At least a dozen times by now."

"I know Mary. But this time is the one time I need to get it right. I know it is him Mary. I can't mess up."

"EL, it is in God's hands. He has brought you together so you need to continue to trust in Him. By the way, what did you decide to wear tonight?"

"I have it narrowed down to 10 outfits. I have tried on about a 100 different ones but can't come up with the right combination. My blue top with yellow shorts. My green top that brings out my eyes. Or my red top that highlights my lips. I have a nice yellow top which is partially see through though it is a little risqué. My brown top is fun but I don't like the way it hangs on my shoulders.

My purple top says HELLO and is too flashy for tonight. My red dress is too sexy for the restaurant. My blue/yellow striped top makes me look fat because the stripes go the wrong way, though it is really cute. My mauve top doesn't have any shorts to go with it and I don't have time to get to the store. My white top is classy but cool, not too sexy, a little see through and shows a little but not too much. If I can't figure this out, I might just end up in my PJs."

"EL. To me it sounds like you should go with your white top."

"Thanks Mary. Now I'll just have to work on what shorts look the best. Wish me luck."

"Good luck EL. And get him in bed."

CHAPTER 13

I knocked on the door when I showed up at EL's apartment. From inside I heard her yell, "the door's open" so I walked into her apartment again. What great memories it brought of three weeks ago.

I wasn't prepared for what I saw though. Just as I got inside, EL came around the corner wearing this deep red dress that seemed to be part of her. It was a perfect match for her deep, deep red hair. All I could do was stare and say "WOW".

After looking at me for what seemed like forever, she walked over, put her finger under by chin and pushed gently to get my mouth to close, gave me one of her kisses on the cheek and whispered into my ear "thanks for the compliment".

She stepped back with a grin that is hard to describe. It was satisfaction, fascination, humor and love all at the same time. In the meantime, her green eyes lit up like she had the whole Milky Way alive inside those eyes. All I could do was continue to stare.

She then gave me the once over and came back up and whispered in my ear again. This time she said "you look wonderful also". She then grabbed my arm, swung me around and said we were off.

As we started to the car, I asked if she was a little over dressed for the Blue Moon West?

She gave me her look, which I absolutely love, and said "I changed my mind. I want to go out clubbing tonight. I was hoping that is OK?"

I'm thinking to myself, a whole night with EL. Dressed like that. I'm in heaven. But all I could get to come out of my mouth was "sure".

And I got that look again from her of "hooked 'em".

"I also thought we would go to Blue Moon East. It is a lot trendier and a little more upscale. Is that OK also?"

All I could say was "sure" again as we got to my car and I opened the door for EL to get in.

CHAPTER 14

The night was both fantastic and a blur. Here is what I remember.

Dinner. The food was great. We must have eaten six or seven different types of sushi, one order at a time. We didn't leave the restaurant until almost 10:00 pm.

We talked about most everything but I'm having a hard time remembering anything specific about her. Whenever I asked about her family, where she was from, or her high school friends, I didn't get much of an answer. I did learn that she has a twin sister named Mary who is living in London.

I also didn't learn much about what she wants to do when she graduates. Everyone I know at the school has these high aspirations of success or service while EL is just, I don't know, just waiting. All it did was make her more intriguing.

After dinner, we headed to two of the nicer clubs in town and had a great time. We laughed, danced, laughed, unsuccessfully tried to talk above the noise, danced some more until surprisingly it was 2:00 am and the clubs were closing. I felt like Cinderella when the clock struck midnight wondering where had the time gone?

When we got back to her place, I walked her up to her apartment.

She asked "do you want to come in for a little bit"?

Oh how I wanted to say yes but I knew that if I went in, I might not come out until Sunday. I told her that I needed to be at Gary's house at 7:00 am to help move one of his friends. I had committed to helping Gary almost a month ago and couldn't let him down.

She said she understood and made me flex my muscles to make sure I would be strong enough to lift boxes in the morning. I promised to give her a call when we were done.

She opened her door, got halfway through the doorway and then turned around. She came over, gave me one of her kisses on the cheek and whispered, "tonight was all I hoped it would be". She headed back into her apartment but not before turning around one more time and giving me a smile that just froze me in place. At the same time, her eyes lit up again.

I headed home thinking I would get a few hours' sleep before needing to head to Gary's house. As you might guess, there was too much swirling around in my brain for me to sleep. All I could do was continue to see that smile, her eyes and that red dress.

Helping Gary's friend move on Saturday was a bitch.

CHAPTER 15

"Mary. Call me as soon as you can. We need to talk. It was fantastic. Tom is fantastic. Life if fantastic. I am fantastic. You are fantastic. God is fantastic. The world is fantastic. Call me."

Ten minutes later.

"EL. What are you doing awake. It must be 3:00 am. And what is it with all this fantastic stuff?"

"Mary. I just had the best night of my life, except maybe for that night in Bethlehem. We talked, we danced, he held me in his arms and sometimes all he could do was stare."

"So did he just leave? Did you two go back to you apartment?"

"Yes he just left. Yes he brought me back to my apartment but he didn't come in. He had to help one of his friends move in 3 hours and thought he needed to head back to his apartment. I think if he would have come in, I might not have let him leave until Sunday."

"So it sounds like you are falling for him EL. You are just supposed to get him into bed."

"I know Mary but there is something special about Tom. Something different. He is a nice guy. I don't know how to explain it Mary. You will just have to meet him for yourself."

"EL. I am glad you had fun but remember our mission. Now tell me all about it. How did he like your white blouse?"

"I didn't wear my white blouse. I wore my red dress. You should have seen his face. I left the door unlocked so when he arrived I told him it was open. He came into the apartment and then I came out of my bedroom in my red dress. I think he injured his jaw when it hit the floor. All I could do was just smile."

"You mean that shit eating grin of yours EL?"

"I'm ignoring that comment Mary. I then walked over, put my finger under his chin, pushed it back in place, gave him a kiss on the cheek and whispered thanks for the compliment. All he could do was stare."

"We then headed out for sushi and talked for two hours over dinner. He is a pretty special guy. Six years in the Air Force as a fighter pilot with three tours in Afghanistan. Both his mother and father have passed away and he doesn't have any brothers or sisters. I could go on and on."

"After dinner we went clubbing. We danced a lot, tried to talk some but the music was too loud and had a lot of fun. Before I knew it, they were saying it was last call and time to go home."

"He drove me home and walked me to my apartment. Like I said earlier, I tried to get him to come in but he already had plans to help his friend move at 7:00 am today."

"So are you going to see him again? Did you just let him leave?" Mary said with as much irritation in her voice as she could muster.

"No. He is going to call me when he is done moving. And then we'll figure it out from there. I think I'm going to invite him over to watch a movie."

"Whatever you do, just get him in bed!"

"Mary. I'm getting there. Remember, patience is a virtue."

"Ok EL but we are trying to save the world. Call me later after you talk with Tom."

"Bye Mary."

CHAPTER 16

"EL. This is Tom. Sorry for calling so late in the afternoon but we are still moving. Gary's friend didn't have everything packed, so we are spending a lot of time just getting them organized. It is pretty frustrating."

"That's OK Tom. Nothing you can do about it. How much longer do you have?"

"My guess is that we will be here until about 7:00 or 8:00 tonight. After that, I'm going to go home, take a hot shower and veg out."

"Are you doing anything special on Monday, Labor Day? Gary's friend is having a thank you barbeque and has invited all of us over for dinner. Do you want to come with me?"

"I'm not going to be a party crasher am I? Are there going to be other girls there?"

"Gary and his friend are both married as is Jeff. Jim has a girlfriend who he should have married three years ago but they both have commitment issues. And you will love Gary's friend's girls. He has two twin girls who are two years old. They are the cutest."

"You are a twin so maybe you can offer some advice on how to raise two girls?"

"I'm not sure that Mary and I are the best example" knowing their childhood was anything but normal.

"So is that a yes that you will join me? If you don't, I'll be the only one there alone."

"Well I would hate for you to have to drink beer and eat barbeque alone. The world may come to an end. So, yes I'll come with you. What time does this start?"

"Monday is supposed to be a beautiful day with temperatures around 80 and the house they are renting has a swimming pool. So they invited everyone over any time after 2:00. It is BYOB and BYOS."

"What is BYOS?"

"Bring your own swimsuit. Hopefully you have one. If not, we'll just throw you into the pool in your clothes."

"Yes I have a swimsuit and you will NOT throw me into the pool. How do you know that I can even swim?"

"Well can you swim?" he asked with a smirk in his voice.

"Yes I can but Mary can't. She never liked the water. Said it was good for drinking and bathing and it crinkles her skin when she goes swimming."

"Hey. Do you golf?"

"No why?"

"Well I'm playing golf tomorrow and we were looking for a fourth. I thought if you golfed, I would invite you."

"Maybe that is something you can teach me. I always thought chasing the ball around was a little silly but I could be persuaded to have an open mind."

"You are too cute."

"What?"

"Nothing. You make me smile. Ok, so we are on for Monday. I'll pick you up at 1:45. We can stop by the grocery store to pick up some drinks and then head over. Sound like a plan?"

"That would be wonderful. Call me tomorrow to double check we are still on. Have fun golfing and don't hurt yourself moving the rest of the boxes."

CHAPTER 17

"Mary, it is EL. He invited me to a barbeque with his friends on Monday. The only thing is that the friend has a swimming pool. You know I hate swimming pools. They make my skin crinkle."

"What did you tell him?"

"I told him that it was you who didn't like to swim and always complained about the water making your skin crinkle."

"EL. How could you? Now he is going to think I'm some kind of weirdo."

"Well, did you want him to think I was some kind of weirdo? I'm trying to get him into bed remember!"

"Ok. I'll take the fall for you this time but try to make me look nice will you?"

"So what kind of swimsuit should I buy? And what color? And where should I go? I have to get this swimsuit in three hours and you know me Mary, I'm not good at making snap decisions about clothes. I like to get lost in the store and think about my options."

"EL. You can go to any of the big box stores. They still have swimsuits. But if I were you, I would go to Nordstrom's. I was in their London store yesterday and they still had a good selection and they were so cute."

"Ooh. Great suggestion. I love shopping there and their staff is always so helpful."

"Well I hate to cut you off EL but you have some shopping to do."

"Thanks Mary. I wouldn't have thought of going there and I know I'll find something that will make Tom's jaw drop."

"Bye EL. And good luck with that swimming pool. Hope your skin doesn't get too crinkly."

As we hung up, all I could hear was Mary laughing.

CHAPTER 18

As I drove over to EL's apartment, I realized I was excited to see her again. It had been less than 48 hours but it seemed like too long. When I got to the apartment, I rang the bell and was surprised when someone other than EL answered the door.

"Hello. You must be Tom. EL has told me all about you. Come on in, she is just about ready. By the way, I am Cindy."

"Hi Cindy. EL told me about what a great roommate you are. It is a pleasure to finally meet you. I thought you weren't coming back until tomorrow?"

"My dad got called to a meeting in New York on Tuesday so he needed to drive me back today so he can catch a flight to New York tomorrow."

Just as she was saying this, her dad came out of the kitchen with a hot cup of coffee. You could still see the steam rising.

"Tom, my name is Jack. I hear you were in the Air Force for a few years. 22 years in the Marines for me. Glad to meet others who have served."

"My dad enjoys meeting other people who have served. He is always telling us that less than 1% of all Americans take time to serve in the Armed Forces."

"I tried to get Cynthia to join the Marines but it just wasn't in her blood. Must have gotten it from her mother's side."

It looked like I was going to be caught in an old family tussle but fortunately EL popped out of her room in time to save me.

"Tom. I'm glad you had the opportunity to meet Cindy and her dad."

"I hope you two don't mind but I think I'm making Tom late for his barbeque plus we still need to stop and get some drinks. We won't be too late since I have a 10:00 am class tomorrow."

"Jack, I'll be quiet when I get home and try not to wake you if are asleep on the couch."

Jack replied, "Don't worry about me. I learned to sleep through just about anything when I'm on friendly ground."

As EL steered me out the door, I said my goodbyes to Jack and Cindy.

On the way to the car, I said "Jack seems like a nice guy" only to be met with the roll of the eyes from EL.

EL shared with me that she really like rooming with Cindy but her dad could be a real pain. He was all about the military and did everything by the books. Up at 5:30 am, to bed at 10:00 pm, breakfast, lunch and dinner always at the same time. He could be sweet if you could get past the regimen. It was interesting having her open up about some of her feelings.

CHAPTER 19

We didn't get to the barbeque until about 2:30. We got lost in the beer section of the grocery store trying to decide what we wanted to drink. We ended up settling on a summer shandy with a little bit of lemon in it. It ended up being the right choice.

By the time we got there, everyone was in the pool and the party was in full swing. EL had on this deep blue bikini that seemed to be made just for her. When she was taking off her clothes to get in the pool, all I could do was stare. She noticed and gave me her standard grin that seemed to convey that satisfaction of having got me again. She walked over, gave me her now patented kiss on the cheek, whispered "thank you" and then she was in the pool.

Quick as a wink, she was at the edge of the pool encouraging me to join her. So off came the outer clothes to reveal my surfing shorts and into the water I went. She forgot to tell me the water was freezing and just chuckled when I complained.

Everyone had fun all afternoon. She spent a lot of time with the twins, teaching them some of the games her and Mary used to play in the pool. It was great watching her, she was going to be a great mom someday and it hurt.

Dinner was everything it was promised to be. Hamburgers, brats, corn on the cob, potato salad, all the fixings and to top it all off - Jim's homemade ice cream. We ended up sitting at a table by ourselves. She shared how much fun she had and how it had been a long time since she had laughed this much.

She also informed me that dinner on Wednesday was at her apartment. When I started to protest, she said that it was her and Cindy's tradition to have a "family" meal every Wednesday at 5:30 pm. They had been doing it since they started rooming together. Cindy's boyfriend/fiancé was going to be in town and she didn't want to be the odd man out. She reminded me that one good turn deserves another.

How could I say no! Another opportunity to spend time with EL.

I ended up dropping her off around 8:30. We both had busy days tomorrow with the first day of classes. And I was going to see her again in my 1:30 pm Information Technology Management class.

I slept well thinking about that blue bikini.

CHAPTER 20

"Hi Mary. What are you doing up so late?"

"I wanted to see how your picnic went. Am I interrupting anything important?"

"No. He just dropped me off and didn't come in with me. We have a busy day tomorrow with it being the first day of class and he is just such a gentleman. Sometimes it is so frustrating."

"Hi Cindy" I said as I came in the door.

"Hi EL" said Cindy. Who are you talking to?"

"I'm talking to Mary."

"Tell her I said hi. When is she coming to visit again? Am I going to get to see her before you graduate?"

"Mary. Cindy says hi. She wants to know when you are coming to visit again?"

"EL. I would be there tomorrow if you would let me."

"Cindy. She doesn't know when but definitely for my graduation."

"EL. How can you tell her that?" Mary said with her protesting voice. I just chose to ignore her.

"And how was the picnic?" Mary asked.

"I went to Nordstrom's like you suggested. They had this too-die-for blue swimsuit. You should have seen Tom's expression when he first saw it. It was precious. This was the second time I got him."

"We had a great time. One of Tom's friends has twin girls age two. I spent time teaching them some of the games we used to play. Tom would watch and had this most interesting look on his face. I'm still trying to figure it out though."

"The food was good, Tom's friends are really nice and I think I got too much sun. Hopefully I won't get too burned. And Tom's friend Jim made homemade ice cream. After a long day in the sun, it really hit the spot. We finished all he made and were giving him a hard time about making more."

"Well what is next on the plan for getting Tom to bed?" Mary asked.

"He is coming over for our Wednesday dinner. You remember that Cindy and I always have a family dinner on Wednesdays. Her boyfriend is coming into town so I invited Tom to join us so I wasn't a third wheel."

"Also, I'm pretty sure he will be in at least one of my classes. I think he has inside information on who is in what class and then makes sure he gets in one of mine. I'll eventually wiggle a confession out of him."

"Well I am beat after a long day in the sun. Let's talk again Wednesday night. I'll give you a call when Tom leaves. We may end up at the library so it might be late. Is that ok?"

"Call me whenever. I can always fall back to sleep."

"Talk with you Wednesday."

CHAPTER 21

Tuesday and Wednesday were good days. EL was in one of my classes each day and she made the effort to sit next to me in both classes. After one day, I could tell the Information Technology Management (IT Man) class was right up my alley. It was also obvious that IT Man was not going to be easy for EL. For some reason she didn't get it but that was a blessing for me. It would allow me to spend a lot of time with her.

Wednesday's dinner was fun. It was EL's turn to cook so she made homemade meatballs to go with our pasta and salad. Maybe I was still star stuck but those were some of the best meatballs ever consumed. Every time I reached for another meatball, she would give me her patented "I gotcha smile".

It was great to meet Cindy's boyfriend/fiancé. He is an artist. By the time dinner was over, I came to realize that he thought about the world so differently. I can't pick out any one thing he said but by the end, I knew that he and I wouldn't hang out too much.

Since EL cooked, it was up to Cindy and her boyfriend to do the cleanup. El and I headed over to the library to work on our IT Man homework.

On the way over to the library, EL asked "tell me about your mom and dad." I stopped, tensed up and gave her what must have been that look of panic. This had been the question that had ultimately been the beginning of the end for all my other romantic relationships and I had been dreading the day it would come.

She must have read me like a book because she did her patented kiss on the cheek and whisper telling me it would be OK. I made a quick prayer that it would, smiled my best smile and said that it was a long story.

In perfect EL fashion, she decided to make it a date. Not sure how it happened but she confirmed me for an afternoon picnic on Saturday. She would bring the fried chicken, I would bring the wine and cheese and we would enjoy the day. She made it all seem ok but inside I was all tied in knots.

I made it through studying that night and the rest of the week. Just barely.

CHAPTER 22

"Hi Mary. Sorry it is so late but Tom and I just finished studying. This IT Management class is going to kick my butt this semester but thankfully it is something that comes easy to Tom. He is a pretty good teacher and with his help, I'm going to do fine."

"How was dinner?"

"Dinner was good. It was my turn to cook so I made meatballs to go with spaghetti. Everyone enjoyed the meal even Cindy's boyfriend. I don't see what she sees in him. But it is her life to live."

"Did you gain any ground with Tom?"

"On the way to the library, I asked about his mom and dad. He froze and turned white. I think I may have hit a raw nerve."

"Soooo?"

"He said it was a long story so I took the opportunity to set another date. We are going on a picnic on Saturday."

"Are you sure he is the right guy EL? Do you think you should accidentally poke him or stab him to verify? I mean, you are putting all this effort into him with no results so far. What if he is the wrong guy?"

"Mary. He is the right guy. I know deep in my heart he is. Your suggestion of poking him though has some merit. I'll think about it."

"EL. This is your last semester at school. If the person we are looking for is there, then you are running out of time. You have put all your eggs in one basket so you better be right."

"You are right. It is time to make sure. I'll do the poke test on Saturday and then let you know."

"Thanks EL. You know I'm here for you. You take care and call me Saturday."

"I will. Bye."

CHAPTER 23

About a block from EL's apartment was a cute little park. We headed over there around 2:00 pm on Saturday with trepidation in my heart. In the past, whenever I told the story of my parents, it was typically the last date and I didn't want this to be the last date.

We got settled in on an Army blanket I brought with me, EL pulled out the chicken and opened a bottle of wine. The chicken was to die for and the wine went well with it. And then EL asked the question, "tell me about your parents". I assumed it was the beginning of the end so I started my tale.

My mom and dad had met in high school and both got jobs without going to college. Dad worked in a factory and mom worked at a college. They didn't make much money and had decided to hold off having children so mom was on birth control.

In their second year of marriage, mom became pregnant with me while still on birth control though my dad didn't believe her. I became the thorn in my dad's side that started his abuse.

After work some days, he would stop at the bars and get drunk. When he got home, him and mom would fight and argue. When I was going to turn eight, my dad kept telling my mom that it was about time for me to become a man and get my first whooping. As my birthday got closer, my dad became more belligerent and my mom became more defensive.

On the night before my birthday, dad was really drunk and started heading my way. Mom grabbed one of the kitchen knives and got between me and dad. When my dad wouldn't stop, mom stabbed him. The courts looked at it as self-defense and mom didn't have to serve any prison time. But it broke her heart. Within a year, she died of a broken heart. I was shipped off to my grandparents who I lived with until I went off to the Air Force.

One thing my grandparents always reminded me of was what mom used to call me. She always said I was her gift from God because she became pregnant when she shouldn't have.

After heading to the Air Force, I decided I never wanted to have any children. I didn't think I could keep my emotions in check so I had a vasectomy done. Without some corrective surgery or another gift from God, I don't plan on being a dad.

"So that is the end of my story" I said. "This is where all my other romantic interests have gotten up and left. It is OK if you want to leave now and not see me again. I'll totally understand."

As I was telling this story, I could see the pain in EL's face and when I was done a single tear ran down her face. She reached out and held my hands for what seemed like the longest time and then she bent over and gave me a kiss. Not the patented kiss on the cheek but a real kiss. I'm not sure what happened but at that moment a peace about my past swept over me. And there in front of my eyes was EL with the most heavenly look I have ever seen in my life.

She didn't say anything other than "I'm sorry and I'll not ask you again. And you won't be able to get rid of me by telling me a story."

We sat there for a long time without saying anything just holding hands. After a while, she offered me a piece of chicken with her smile.

We got to laughing and talking about other things, mainly school, as I was cutting the cheese. Somehow I ended up poking myself and started bleeding.

EL said "let me kiss it and make it better".

I looked at her and asked if she really wanted to tempt fate again, reminding her that the last time she did, she almost ended up in the ER.

She talked about how stressed she was last time and how it was a fluke and couldn't happen again. So I presented my figure to her so she could kiss it and make it better.

Next thing I know, EL is passed out on my lap but just for a second or two this time. As she was coming back around and somewhere between passed out and fully awake, I saw the most magnificent look in her eyes. It was the look I always imagined I would see if I was looking at an angel. It passed as panic set it.

I'm not sure who was more worried, EL or me. She started apologizing for passing out and I could only keep asking her if she was ok.

Finally, we both started to calm down and then EL started laughing. And then she reached up, gave me this wonderful kiss and said thank you.

I'm not really sure what she meant but I took the moment to give her a kiss back and say she was crazy. To which she said "yes I am".

She just laid there in my lap for what seemed like forever until she said she still wanted some cheese and that I needed to finish the last piece of chicken. And just like that, the spell was broken.

CHAPTER 24

We had finished her chicken and were half way done with the wine when she asked "can I tell you about my family"? I said sure but could see the angst in her face.

My sister and I lived on a farm with my parents and Grandfather. He grew the best fruit around. People would come from miles around to buy his fruits. He called his farm The Garden.

Near the house was this tiny tree that produced about 20 pieces of fruit per year. Grandfather used to call it the Healing Tree. Each piece of fruit would fetch a king's ransom but he never sold them. He would pick out 19 people who were struggling with their health and invite them to The Garden. He would then share a piece of fruit with each of them. They would go home and over the course of time, each would recover from their ailments. He would reserve one piece for us all to share, just so we could remember each year the value of the tree.

The summer we were six, mom and dad got possessed by something and one evening they ate half of the fruit on the tree. When grandfather saw what they had done, he said they would have to leave the farm. The next morning he sent them packing.

When it was time to leave, my parents said they didn't want to take Mary and me with them. They didn't know where they were going or how they would support us. Grandfather said that would be OK so they left promising to come back and get us. They never did.

Mary and I grew up in The Garden and helped grandfather. He taught us how to be ladies, how to respect the earth and how to get along in the world.

When she was done telling the story, my heart was breaking for her. Now I knew why she hadn't run away after my story. All I could do was reach over and give her that same warm kiss she had given me. In that moment, we became one.

We spent the rest of the afternoon talking about everything and talking about nothing. When we got back to her apartment, I came in to help clean up after our picnic and put things away. When I went to leave, EL said "what does a girl like me have to do to get a boy like you to spend the night with her"?

I was taken a little by surprise and gave kind of flippant answer of "you are just going to have to marry me."

And in a similar voice EL said "well then I'll consider your proposal". I didn't think anything about it as I gave her a kiss good night and headed back to my place.

CHAPTER 25

"Mary. Good news, bad news and great news. What do you want first?"

"Sandwich the bad news in between the great news and good news."

"So here is the great new. Tom is definitely the one."

"How did you figure that out EL?"

"On our picnic today, he was cutting some cheese and poked himself. I said I would kiss it and make it better and he gave me some sarcastic remark like 'you aren't going to pass out on me are you?'"

"I gave him my best death look and he offered up his finger with a smile. Next thing I know, I'm waking up in his arms again. Mary, I knew it was coming and I still got hammered. The good news is that I was only out for a second or two this time."

"EL. That is fantastic. So all my worries about you chasing the wrong person have been in vain."

"I think I gave away a little though when I was waking up. You know that fleeting moment between asleep and awake when we are vulnerable to be seen? Tom was looking straight into my eyes and I think he saw. He didn't say anything but I saw that look cross his face."

"What are you going to do about it? Is this the bad news? If so, that's not so bad."

"I'm going to ignore the look and never bring it up. And that is not the bad news."

"Well what is the bad new?"

"I got him talking about his parents. It is a sad story that we can talk about in more detail later. But the short version is that his dad was abusive so when he joined the Air Force, he had a vasectomy done because he didn't want to have children and be like his dad."

"Um EL. That is really bad news. How do you get his seed if he has it blocked?"

"I'm not sure Mary. We need to be praying and asking God for a miracle. He has us on a mission and I have faith he will provide the answer."

"I'm with you there EL. Prayer it is. So what is the good news?"

"Remember I told you that I haven't been having any success in getting him to spend the night? So I asked him, 'what does it take for a girl like me to get a boy like you to spend the night?'"

"You didn't really ask him that did you EL?"

"You bet I did. I didn't know what else to do."

"So what did he say?"

"He made an offhand comment about 'well you are going to have to marry me.'"

"And what did you say to that?"

"I said that I would consider his proposal. I'm not sure that he took my answer too seriously because I used the same flippant tone of voice he did."

"After this, he gave me a kiss and headed back to his apartment."

"So what are you going to do?"

"Next Saturday when we go do something, I am going to accept his proposal. We will be getting married the day after graduation so make your travel plans now. I want you to be my Maid of Honor."

"Does he know this?"

"Not yet but we'll get there. If that is the only way to get him to sleep with me, then marriage it is. Besides Mary, I really like Tom. He is sweet. He treats me with respect, honor and love. I can see me married to him for a long time."

"Are you sure? You know the longer you are married, the longer before conception. I'm not sure the world can wait that long."

"It will just have to wait. I have been praying a lot about this and I always get a sense of peace when I ask the Lord about it. Maybe the extra time is part of his plan. I just don't know."

"Well EL. I'll start praying about this also. Any other revelations you want to dump on me tonight? You know it is 2:00 am here in London and with all you shared with me, I won't be getting any sleep tonight. Too much thinking and too much praying. Thanks!" she said in a very sarcastic tone.

"Mary. Thanks for being here for me. You know I won't be able to make it through without you. You are the bestest sister ever. And I love you to the moon and back."

"I love you to EL. Call me if you have any answered prayers and I'll call you if I get any."

"Sleep well Mary" I said with too big of a smile on my face.

CHAPTER 26

It was another hard week. We were two-thirds of the way through the semester which meant is was getting to be crunch time. Of my four classes, two of them had me working with groups to create our group presentation, one had me working on my semester paper and the other had me spending 10 hours per week working as an intern at one of the start-ups that routinely spun out of the college.

EL was in a similar crunch. She had three group presentation that she was working on and one paper.

Even though we had a lot to do, we still saw each other every day either in school or meeting at the library. Wednesday was still family dinner night with the two of us and Cindy. They made me cook once early on only to see that I wasn't the best. Since then, they left me out of the cooking rotation and assigned me to clean up detail. They did let me bake every now and then, as that is something my grandmother had taught me.

Saturday came as one of those truly memorable late autumn days. The high was going to be around 55 degrees, the sun was warm but the wind promised the beginnings of winter.

EL and I decided it would be a nice day to check out the botanical gardens. They had a mix of outdoor and indoor gardens so we would wonder outside for a while until we got cold and would then head back inside.

On our third trip back inside, we were sitting next to this pretty little fountain. EL was holding my arm as she liked to do and looked at me and said "Yes".

"Yes, what?" I asked back.

"Yes. I have decided to accept your offer."

"What offer?"

"The offer you made last week, of course" she said.

"What offer did I make last week?" I asked totally confused.

"Don't you remember last week when I asked how a girl like me could get a guy like you to spend the night with me? And you said and I quote "you are just going to have to marry me", end quote. Well I have spent all week considering your proposal and I accept."

"I do want the whole kneeling on one knee and ring thing to make it official but Yes!"

After a short pause, she finished with "and please don't make me wait too long."

All kinds of thoughts were racing through my head. One was, how lucky a guy I was. Another was, did I just get engaged? Then, where did this come from? And how lucky a guy I was. Followed by holy crap. And a ring? And where should I officially propose and how? And did I say how lucky a guy I was?

I looked over at EL and there she sat so serenely with that smile on her face.

All I could do was give her the most passionate kiss we ever had.

We didn't talk about much the rest of the afternoon or maybe it is that I don't remember much more of the afternoon. I do remember being on cloud nine. And almost being engaged!

CHAPTER 27

"Mary. We went to the botanical gardens today. They are so beautiful. We'll have to go to them when you are in town."

"EL. When am I coming to town?"

"And I said yes to Tom today and got a wonderful kiss in return."

"What did you say yes to?"

"To Tom's offer of course."

"What did Tom offer?"

"I can't believe I am having the same conversation with you that I had with him. Don't you remember our conversation from last weekend? Did you forget already that I'm going to get married?"

"EL. I thought you were pulling my leg. Did he propose to you?"

"NOOOOOO."

"EL. It is ok. Start from the beginning please."

"Mary. Remember that I can't get Tom to sleep with me. And remember that I point blank asked what I needed to do to get him to sleep with me. And also remember that he made the flippant comment about 'you'll just have to marry me'. Do you remember all that?"

"Yes I do EL."

"Well, while we were at the botanical gardens, I told him yes. He asked 'yes what' and we had the same conversation you and I just had until he finally got it. Do you get it?"

There was a long pause and then Mary asked "Did he buy that story? Did he propose?"

"To use your words, he bought that story. He hasn't officially proposed but I told him I wouldn't wait too long."

"So when is the wedding?"

"Mary. Don't you remember anything from last weekend?"

"Well it was 2:00 am and I had just gotten back from a tough night at the pubs."

"You are beyond belief Mary. So the wedding is going to be the day after graduation and you are going to be my Maid-of-Honor. BOOK YOUR TICKETS!" I said, hopefully with enough force to get it to stick in her brain this time.

"Ok. Ok. You don't need to yell."

"I need it to stick this time. I need you to help me get ready for my wedding. I need your support Mary."

"EL. I support you 120%. You know that. So changing subjects. Did you get any answered prayers?"

"No answered prayers yet though I know they will come. I still have a peace about this wedding Mary and feel it is the right thing. I know God will let me know what to do next."

"So how many days before the wedding do you want me to come? I could come now and we could have a great time."

"Mary. If you come now, I'll never get engaged. Nor will I ever graduate. We'll spend all our time at the bars and no time at the library. That is not the image I am trying to portray to Tom. Can you come one week before the wedding? That would be December 8th. Graduation is December 15th and we'll get married on the 16th."

"What if Tom doesn't propose in time?"

"Let me worry about that."

"Ok EL. Tom is in your hands and I will start wedding dress shopping over here. I'm thinking Nordstrom's again since we each have one. Does that work for you?"

"Yes it does. You know what I like. Also, I want you to wear a black dress with some white in it. Does that work for you?"

"Yes, that works for me. I'll text you my ideas."

"Sounds like we have a plan. Now I need to work on Tom."

"Yes you do EL. Work! Work! Work!"

"Thanks for being here for me. You know I won't make it through this without you."

"I'm here for you EL. And you have done this enough times before to not need me."

"I always need you Mary."

"You flatter me because you want me to do the hard work of picking out a dress. But I'm willing to help. I'll talk with you later in the week."

"Ok Mary. Thanks again!"

CHAPTER 28

I didn't sleep well Saturday night. Too much on my mind. EL saying yes to my non-proposal. Me being the luckiest man on the planet. How to propose to her and when? Where to get married and when? Who to ask to be my best man since I have three of them? Weird dreams. I think I woke up Sunday more tired than when I went to bed.

I needed some guy help so I called my brain trust of Jim, Jeff and Gary. I promised them free coffee at Starbucks if they would meet me there at 1:00 pm after church. They all agreed especially since I was buying.

When everyone was there, had their coffee and got done harassing me about buying, "as a note – I never buy", we got down to business. I swore them to secrecy and each agreed to not tell anyone until they left Starbucks, which was the best I was probably going to get.

I filled them in on my Saturday and each of them were laughing up a storm when I was done and passing money between them. I couldn't believe they were laughing and betting until Jeff shared that they had a pool going on when I was going to get engaged and who was going to ask who. It looked like Gary got closest to the date and Jim was the only one picking EL. So Jeff got cleaned out.

When I asked for advice on how to propose, I got more recommendations than the law allows. They suggested a hot air balloon (too cold), scuba diving (she isn't a fan of water), putting it in a cupcake (not a sweets person), painting The Fence (I liked this one but I remember a comment from EL about how childish that was) and renting a plane with one of those trailing signs (too expensive). We settled on dinner at Blue Moon East which is where we had our first date. Hokie but romantic all at the same time.

My brain trust then started about how big the ring should be, the different types of cuts, etc. After 10 minutes of suggestions and more ribbing, I shared that I had my mother's wedding ring. Before she passed away, that was all she had left. She had begged me not to bury it with her and to keep it as a reminder of her love for me. I think I saw a tear in Gary's eyes though he wouldn't admit to it.

So it was settled, after two cups of coffee along with some muffins, that the proposal would be Friday at Blue Moon East using my mother's ring. I left with peace of mind and a plan.

Now all I had to do was get to Friday. Easier said than done.

CHAPTER 29

Whenever I saw EL during the week, she had that expectant look though she never said a word. Friday I went to pick her up for our date and she looked stunning. She had found a blue dress that was a perfect match for the swimming suit she had worn over Labor Day. When I asked if they matched, she just smiled her killer smile.

I hadn't told her where we were going but somehow she had known to dress appropriately. I wondered if she got to my brain trust and weaseled out the location for our dinner from one of them. It was probably Jim.

I had reached out to the owner of the Blue Moon East earlier in the week to let him know I was going to propose to EL. I found out he was a romanticist so he arranged the perfect table for us, just slightly away from everyone else. He also said to be ready around 9:00 pm and he would do something special.

Right on cue at 9:00, the lights flickered a little bit in the restaurant, all the waiters asked each of the tables to be quiet and a hush, that I didn't think was possible, came over the restaurant. It was my time to do my thing.

I stood up and went around the table to EL. Down on one knee, I proposed to her and guess what. She said Yes.

After a big kiss from me and some cheering from the crowd, we settled back into our dinner. She was impressed that I was able to pull off something this nice.

She asked me about the ring and where I got it because she could tell it wasn't new. I told her it was my mom's ring. It was the only thing of value she had left when she passed away and asked me to keep it instead of burying it with her. By the end of the story, EL had tears coming down her cheeks. She said she was honored to wear the ring and would always treasure it.

I asked if she had thought about the wedding, when she wanted to have it and where. She talked about having it the day after graduation at our church with a very small service. Neither of us had family other than EL's sister. Our real family were our friends from school and it would be nice to have them at the wedding. By having it right after graduation, they could easily stick around for an extra day before we all went our separate ways. I couldn't argue with her logic so it was decided.

She said that Mary would be her Maid-of-Honor and wanted to know who my best man was. I shared that I didn't know who to pick from Gary, Jim and Jeff. She saw I was struggling with my decision so she recommended that I ask all three of them to be my best men. I would see over the years that this was one of her strengths, seeing clarity in the moment and making great recommendations. So it was decided that I would have three best men.

It was an evening we would both remember and talk about frequently over the years. I thought it was the best night of my life but that was still to come.

CHAPTER 30

When I answered the phone, all I could hear was EL screaming. I think she broke my eardrum with the screech that was coming through the phone. It took me forever to get her calmed down before I could understand anything she said.

Mary, she screamed. "I'm engaged. I'm engaged. I'm engaged. He proposed. He proposed. He proposed." That was all she was saying for almost a minute.

EL's excitement was infectious and I started jumping up and down also. The folks in the coffee shop gave me the look of 'weirdo' so I yelled out to everyone "she's engaged" and everyone applauded. When EL calmed down a little more and I was finally able to get a word in edgewise, I said "tell me about it. I want to hear all the gory details. And start from the beginning instead of the middle."

"Starting from the beginning. A year and a half ago, I started at the university."

"Not there you moron. The beginning of last night."

"Well I was just doing what you asked."

"Don't be a smart-aleck. It doesn't fit you."

"So Tom came to pick me up around 7:30 last night. I had this blue dress that was the same color as the swimsuit I had worn on Labor Day. It was killer. When Tom saw it, his jaw hit the floor and I was able to give him a kiss on the cheek and thank him for the compliment. He is getting a lot of practice with the jaw hitting the floor and I am enjoying it."

"He took me to Blue Moon East, which is where I took him for my thank you dinner. We were having an enjoyable dinner at a table set apart from the crowd. When we sat down, I thought how good our timing was to get this cute little table. Little did I know that Tom had schemed with the owner before our arrival."

"At 9:00 pm, this hush came over the restaurant. I didn't think a restaurant could get that quiet and I was thinking how odd that was, and then Tom was beside me on one knee. It took a few seconds for it all to click and I almost missed Tom asking me to marry him. Of course I said yes and give him a very passionate kiss to which we got a standing ovation from almost the entire restaurant."

"It was magical Mary. I didn't think he could pull it off but he exceeded my expectations."

"EL. That is so sweet. It sounds like he worked really hard to make it special. What kind of ring did he get? Is it a huge one?"

"The ring is this little dingy, beat-up ring that is better than any ring he could have purchased. It was his mom's ring. As Tom tells the story, it was the last thing of value she had when she died and she had begged Tom not to bury it with her. She wanted him to remember her with love. For him to share that with me and want me to wear it means so much."

"EL. You have me crying over here."

"I was crying also when he told the story. Mary, I can't wait for you to meet him."

"So did he buy off on your plan to get married right after graduation?"

"He did. He thinks it is a great plan. I told him you were going to be my Maid-of-Honor. When I asked who he was going to pick for his best man, he struggled between his three best friends. So I made the command decision that he would have three best men, allowing him to not have to choose."

"So I get to hang out with three eligible bachelors?"

"Unfortunately no. Two of them are married and one is involved in a long term relationship which you are not allowed to tamper with!"

"You are no fun EL. Who am I going to hang with?"

"We decided on about 12 people to invite to the wedding and three of them are eligible bachelors. Two of them are really cute and one is kind of nerdy but really nice. Can't wait to see which one you choose."

"EL, I'm so happy for you. It has been a long, long time since I've seen you this excited. I don't mean to be a buzz-kill but remember the mission."

"You are a buzz-kill but I won't let you ruin this moment. I love you Mary and can't wait to see you. Any success on the dress?"

"I have been looking but nothing that tickles my fancy yet. I need to run. My coffee is cold and my pastry is dry and hard. I love you too EL and can't wait to see you also. Call me early next week. Bye."

CHAPTER 31

Monday we were studying and I asked EL "how did you get your name? It is so unique."

In a second, I could see panic come across her face. It was the same look I gave her when she asked about my mom and dad. So I tried out an EL-ism. I leaned over, gave her a kiss on the cheek and whispered "I love you" and went back to studying. EL put her hand in mine and squeezed gently as if to say thank you.

About five minutes later, she took this big breath and started to tell me her story.

"As you know, my sister and I were raised on a farm. My parents were a little strange, so when we were born, they named us the letters L and M. They thought it was so cute and so did we until we had to interact with other kids our age. We go teased a lot."

"Mary and I made a pact that I would start calling her Mary and she would call me Liz. We made up some story to tell the kids about our real names and frankly I don't remember the story. I do know this stopped the teasing."

"When I got into high school, there were a couple girls named Liz who were terrible people and I didn't want to be associated with them. Mary and I worked on names and we finally settled on EL."

"I know it is a stupid story. All because my parents were weird."

"I think it is a beautiful name EL. I am excited to get to call you EL for the rest of our lives together. I will be especially respectful of the name and you will never hear me teasing you."

She leaned over and gave me one of her patented kisses on the cheek and whispered "thanks".

CHAPTER 32

Wednesday was wedding preparation day. The three of us had scheduled two hours to work through our plan and Cindy was the stand-in for Mary from a maid-of-honor perspective.

EL and I had talked with the church and our minister on Tuesday and they were fine with us having the wedding on December 18th. Since it was a Sunday, our wedding couldn't start until after 2:00 pm when all the church activities were complete. We decided on a 4:00 pm wedding and a 5:00 pm dinner.

The three of us worked through our guest list and we ended up with 17 people to invite. With EL and me, the wedding party would total 19 people.

Our next decision was where to have the wedding dinner. My suggestion was Blue Moon East but EL reminded me that they closed on Sundays after serving lunch. We knocked around another dozen or so places without finding one that we loved. We even talked about having it catered to the church.

I asked if I could take a break and make a quick call and got the evil eye from both EL and Cindy. I just did an eye roll back at them and they said "Sure" very sarcastically.

I went outside and called the owner of the Blue Moon East. We had become semi-friends when I was scheming with him on my proposal. I told him of our desire to have the wedding dinner at his place. He explained that they closed on Sundays at 2:00 pm. I thanked him for his time and headed back inside.

The girls were deep into what colors to use for the wedding, what type of invitations to send, whether it was OK to hand deliver them since everyone was local or should they still mail them.

I asked the trivia question on why there are two envelopes used in the wedding invitations and guess what? I stumped the ladies. Neither of them knew the reason. Feeling all full of myself I preceded to tell them that in the old days, think medieval times, letters were carried in saddle bags from town to town and could take weeks to get somewhere. The letters usually arrived with a fair amount of grime on them, so the custom became to put a second envelope inside the first so when presented to the lady of the house, she was opening a clean envelope.

Cindy thought I was pulling the wool over her eyes so she immediately brought up Bing and did a search. The answer she found online was essentially what I told her. She still wouldn't give me credit though for having it right. Just a lucky guess on my part.

We were just about to wrap up when my phone rang. I answered and it was the owner of Blue Moon East. He had talked to his wife and they were calling back to say they would be honored if they could host our wedding party.

I shared this quickly with EL and Cindy and they both said yes. EL even got up and did the happy dance. I told the owner how excited we were and thanked him.

EL asked me how he knew we wanted to have our wedding party there. I said it must have been a God thing and then she remembered me walking out to make a call and gave me a slug on the shoulder followed by a kiss of thanks. My shoulder hurt but the blow was softened by the kiss.

With most of the plans complete and our time all used up, it was back to the grind of studying. All three of us had plenty to do so EL and I headed for the library and our study groups just as Cindy's group was showing up.

CHAPTER 33

"Mary, I have good new and great news. Which do you want to hear first?" I asked Thursday morning on my way to class.

"Start with the good news and finish with the great news."

"So the good news is that we finished the wedding plans last night. Cindy did an admirable job of filling in for you, being eccentric and asking the stupid questions." I said with a chuckle.

"Cute EL. Are you sure you want me to be your Maid-of-Honor?"

"Well yes I want you to be my Maid-of-Honor. Who else would it be?" I answered sarcastically. I was feeling chipper today and letting Mary know it.

"So give me the short version of the plans."

"Total guests not including Tom and me are 19. There are three eligible bachelors for you to pick from. Our color is purple of course. The wedding is at 4:00 and dinner is at 5:00."

"Wonderful. Where is the dinner being held?"

"That is a neat story. Tom and I both wanted it to be the Blue Moon East. That is where we had our first date and where he proposed but it closes on Sunday at 2:00 pm. We talked about another dozen or so places but just couldn't decide. Tom asked if he could take a break and make a call. He called the owner who he worked with on the proposal. About 45 minutes later, the owner called back and said that he and his wife would be honored to host our wedding dinner. Isn't that sweet?"

"That is very sweet. Did you know Tom was calling the owner."

"No we didn't. And we gave him the evil eye when he asked to make the call. He is the bestest."

"You know that isn't a word don't you?"

"I do but it really describes him. Maybe if I use it enough, we can make it a new word. What do you think?"

"Never going to happen EL. But as long as you are happy, you can keep on using it. So if that is the good news, what is the great news?"

"The great news. You know how we have been struggling with Tom's vasectomy? Well an angel came to me last night. She said that I would have the power to heal on my wedding night. It came with a warning though of long term consequences without restraint. I'm not sure what that means though and as usual, there aren't any further directions."

"Wow." Followed by a long pause. "That is great news but I wonder what it means. I'll think on it and we can talk more when I get there."

"Thanks Mary. I woke up with a calm and peace about me with a little bit of nagging fear. We definitely need to talk through this over a beer. Can't wait to see you in two weeks."

"Unless something earth shattering occurs, I'm probably not going to call. I have two papers to complete, one presentation and one final to study for. I'll be spending most of my time in class or at the library."

"And with Tom" Mary added with a chuckle.

"And with Tom" I said with a big smile on my face.

CHAPTER 34

EL and I went to pick up Mary at the airport. It was one of those crisp, mid-December days with the promise of snow the next day. Mary's flight from London connected in Chicago where winter had already arrived so she was running three hours late.

EL had been fretting but I had learned there is nothing you can do about the airlines. The best remedy is to have a good book on hand, a cup of coffee to drink and no expectations. With these plans, it makes it easy to roll with the good and bad travel experiences.

It was finally time and Mary came through security. I had to take a double take to make sure that EL was still standing next to me because it was eerie how much they looked alike. The thought that ran through my head was, boy they could really mess with people by substituting one for the other.

After hugs between the girls, EL turned to introduce Mary to me and the second eerie moment occurred. Mary gave me the same once over that I always get from EL before we go out followed by a kiss on the cheek. Only Mary kissed on the right cheek while EL always kissed on the left cheek. Over Mary's stay, Mary was consistent on which cheek got kissed by whomever she kissed.

On the way home from the airport, Mary wanted the driving tour to get a visual image of the stories EL had been telling her. We drove past the botanical gardens first and the girls made a mental date to get there on Monday after class.

Next was Blue Moon East where we stopped for a quick lunch and to introduce Mary to the owners. During our lunch, they kept stopping by and saying "So alike" to Mary and EL. On the third trip by, they showed us some pictures of their four children, two of which were identical twins also. It made for great story telling.

From there we drove on to the campus and did a quick walking tour. Mary wanted to see the library where it all began. We whispered the tale at the table while Mary and EL kept exchanging weird glances at each other. I took it that it was just them being together for the first time in a while.

Finally, we drove past my apartment on the way to EL's apartment. Cindy surprised us by making lasagna while we were gone so I ran out to the store to pick up some garlic bread and beer while Mary and EL got settled in.

Dinner was a hoot as we got Mary telling some of her stories from the past year in Australia and London. I came to realize that she was a pretty free spirit, so much different than EL.

As I headed home that night, the promised snow was just beginning. Mary had fallen asleep on the couch and EL made me promise to call when I arrived home so I checked in upon successfully getting home. I had a big day tomorrow, finishing up two papers and one presentation.

CHAPTER 35

"Mary. Wake up. Tom has left and Cindy has gone to bed. We need to talk."

"I'm awake. Let's go into your room so we aren't overheard" she said in a whisper.

As we headed into the bedroom, Mary asked "How did you like the dress I picked out? Is it going to be OK? It is a little provocative but I really wanted to make sure that something happened after the wedding. By the way, where are you honeymooning?"

"We are going to take our honeymoon after Christmas on our way to our new jobs. Tom needs to be at his new job on January 4th and so do I. We are thinking of heading down to the Florida Keys to enjoy some sunshine and diving. You know that is one of my favorite places" as they both plopped down on EL's bed.

"I know you love the Keys but you are going to have to remember to play dumb about being there and its history."

"Yeah, that's right. I'll be careful."

"But where are you going for the evening of your wedding? Seriously, where is all the action going to take place?"

"Tom has booked the penthouse suite at the Marriott for Sunday and Monday evening. It supposedly has 800 square feet of living space. I told him that I wasn't planning on coming out of the suite and to be prepared. He and room service are going to be my sustenance for 36 hours."

"What was Tom's reaction?"

"A big, shit-eating grin was all he could manage. And that is all I wanted to see" she said with the same grin on her face.

"He has already paid for the room and they will have the key ready for us around 8:00 pm. I can't wait."

"So have you been thinking about the vision? What do you think it means?"

"I'm not sure Mary. I have racked my brain thinking how am I going to heal his vasectomy and I can't conceive of how it will happen. What have you been thinking?"

"EL. I can't think of anything either. It is not like you are going to have a lot to work with. You are both going to be naked, in a room alone with no medical assistance. I know God has a plan but I sure hate it when he doesn't share."

"You and me both. I have all the faith that it will happen though."

"What do you think of the warning EL? How can there be long term consequences. Once you get the seed, you can leave him."

"Mary. I love Tom. I want to spend the rest of his life with him. I can't marry him today and divorce him tomorrow. That wouldn't be right and you know it. It would crush him."

"EL. You have to leave him though. It is time!" she said a little too forcefully.

"Well what if the right time is after Tom dies? What if God's plan included me falling in love with him? How do we know?"

"We don't know EL. You are right about that but you can't wait too long. I know you think you love him but the world needs your child more."

"Thanks Mary" she said frustrated. "I know you love me but over these past months, I've come to see Tom's heart and it is the purest heart I have had the opportunity to see. Hopefully you will see this also during the week."

"I'll keep an eye out for it. He does seem sweet and I like his smile. Can we share?"

"No we can't share Mary. That has never worked before and even though we are identical in looks, we aren't the same in demeanor. So NO sharing. Got it?"

"You are such a party pooper EL. But I'll honor your request" Mary conceded. "Now tell me how do you like the dress?"

"Oh Mary. It is beautiful. I am so excited to wear it. I tried it on and it fit perfectly. I can't wait to see Tom's look. He has this wonderfully cute stare with his jaw open and I love coming up to him and gently pushing under his chin. Instead of watching me when I come in, watch Tom for the look. It is so precious."

"I will be watching and I'll make sure the camera man has two cameras so we get the look. Now I have got to get some sleep EL. It has been a really long day. What are we doing tomorrow?"

"Tomorrow you are on your own until 3:00 pm. I have two study groups to wrap up our projects and have about an hour's worth of work to finish my paper. I'll be out of here around 8:00 am and home by 3:00."

"We won't see Tom tomorrow, because he has more left to do than I do and he wants to be done tomorrow also. If we can get through tomorrow, the only thing left is a test on Thursday for both of us, which you can help me study for."

"I am so glad you are here Mary. It has been way too long apart."

As Mary was falling asleep, I heard her say "sure. Love you too" which is what we always have said to each other.

I whispered "sure. Love you too" also.

CHAPTER 36

Wednesday was our last family dinner. With the semester coming to a close, EL and I would be heading out of town. Cindy was also graduating and was hoping to move in with her boyfriend and find a job in Pittsburgh. As a special treat, Mary offered to make us an Australian dish with lamb and vegetables along with some mashed potatoes on the side.

Mary recruited me for doing some of the preparation of the vegetables and as I was cutting, I accidentally poked myself. Out of habit, EL said "let me kiss it and make it better" to which both Cindy and I almost screamed NO!

EL was taken a little aback but recovered. She looked at Cindy who said "don't look at me. I'm not kissing it to make it better. I've seen what it did to you."

This was the perfect opening for Mary. She said that it was their family tradition and so she would give it a kiss. There was some unspoken communication that went between EL and Mary which I couldn't make out, to which Mary said she would be OK.

So I dutifully put out my finger so she could kiss it and make it better. No sooner had my finger touched her lips and I was diving to catch Mary, whose head was heading towards the corner of the counter, because she passed out. I was able to save her but took a pretty nasty poke in the shoulder when I got between Mary and the counter.

There I sat now with Mary in my arms just like my first experience with EL. Mary was out for about 30 second and just as she was coming around, in the split second between unconsciousness and consciousness, I saw that same angelic look I had seen in EL the second time she passed out. This time I was much surer of the look having seen it before.

Before I could say anything, EL and Cindy were fussing with Mary. Cindy was saying that she was glad that she hadn't kissed my finger and this was even more proof that there was something wrong with me. EL was worried about Mary and if she had hurt herself, only to find out only her pride was hurt. And again I saw a strange look pass between the two of them.

We got Mary to the couch along with a good stiff shot of scotch. Cindy was saying we should call 911 but both EL and Mary said she would be OK. Cindy backed down but only after a lot of convincing.

With Mary now out of commission, the Australian lamb dinner was not going to happen so we ordered pizza. I picked it up along with some fresh beers.

It was an eventful last family supper, one that EL and I would talk about over the years. And it was a great time to enjoy our favorite pizza one last time.

CHAPTER 37

After Tom left and Cindy had headed to bed, Mary and I began to talk.

"Holy crap EL. You didn't warn me that it was that strong."

"Mary. I told you that I have passed out twice now. The second time I knew it was coming and it still sent me for a loop. How much more warning do you need?"

"Obviously, I wasn't listening hard enough. Now I understand what you mean and why you have focused solely on Tom. I have never been walloped like that. Ever!"

"So now you finally believe me, ah? Did you think I have been making this up?"

"EL, I always believed you. Now I BELIEVE you."

After a long pause, Mary asked "Didn't you say something about him seeing through to your soul the second time you passed out?"

"Yeh. Why?"

"I'm pretty sure he was looking into my eyes in the brief instance when I was waking up and saw. He had this look of recognition come across his face. And I think he was going to say something but you and Cindy were fussing so much, that he wasn't able to."

"I sure hope he doesn't ask Mary. I'm not sure what I'll tell him. You know we can't tell him anything."

"Yes I know. Fortunately, the week is only going to get more hectic so I don't think it will come up. It will come up some time in the future, so start thinking of an answer."

"I also see why you like him EL. When I was waking, I saw his look of love. If you weren't going to be marrying him, I sure would be. You can see straight into his soul through those blue eyes."

EL didn't respond but just smiled and shook her head up and down.

They talked for another hour before both were tired and ready to sleep. EL said "I love you" to which Mary said "sure, I love you too."

CHAPTER 38

Sunday came crisp and clear. The sun was shining and the butterflies were everywhere, including in my stomach.

I was standing at the front of the church with Jeff, Gary and Jim, waiting for the service to begin. We were talking with the minister when we got the cue that it was time to start.

First to come down the aisle was Mary in a simple, plain black dress. She definitely got the attention of all the males at the wedding until EL turned the corner to walk down.

Over the past months, she had stunned me a few times with the beauty of her clothes but nothing prepared me for today. I'm not sure how she did it, but it was like the dress had been made specifically for her. It made me think of a few Disney princesses.

As she walked up the aisle, all I could do was stare at her radiant beauty. The closer she got the bigger her smile got as she saw my reaction to her. When she finally go to me, she put her finger under my chin and pushed gently, gave me her patented kiss on the cheek and whisper "thanks".

At that moment, I was so grateful that the minister had made us practice the night before. I was able to function on instinct instead of having to think.

EL had designed the service to be simple but elegant and that is what is was. In looking back at the video, I don't think it could have been any more perfect. EL's favorite part of wedding services has always been the Bible reading of 1 Corinthians 13.

> *If I speak in the tongues of men or of angels, but do not have love, I am only a resounding gong or a clanging cymbal. 2 If I have the gift of prophecy and can fathom all mysteries and all knowledge, and if I have a faith that can move mountains, but do not have love, I am nothing. 3 If I give all I possess to the poor and give over my body to hardship that I may boast, but do not have love, I gain nothing.*

> *4 Love is patient, love is kind. It does not envy, it does not boast, it is not proud. 5 It does not dishonor others, it is not self-seeking, it is not easily angered, it keeps no record of wrongs. 6 Love does not delight in evil but rejoices with the truth. 7 It always protects, always trusts, always hopes, always perseveres.*

8 Love never fails. But where there are prophecies, they will cease; where there are tongues, they will be stilled; where there is knowledge, it will pass away. 9 For we know in part and we prophesy in part, 10 but when completeness comes, what is in part disappears. 11 When I was a child, I talked like a child, I thought like a child, I reasoned like a child. When I became a man, I put the ways of childhood behind me. 12 For now we see only a reflection as in a mirror; then we shall see face to face. Now I know in part; then I shall know fully, even as I am fully known.

13 And now these three remain: faith, hope and love. But the greatest of these is love.

After about 10 minutes, we got to my two favorite parts of the wedding. The first is where we get to say "I do". I know I'm almost done at that point. And the second is where the minister says "you may kiss the bride". I now know we are done and this is where the work begins.

In my mind, our kiss lasted forever and was the most passionate kiss ever known to man, because this was the kiss of true love. It would foretell of many stories to come.

From the church, we headed over to Blue Moon East, where we were treated like royalty. Never had a feast been served better than the one we ate that night. Our friends enjoyed themselves and the dinner would be a point of conversation for years to come.

At long last, the time came for EL and me to leave. I know I left with joy and anticipation in my heart. We thanked everyone for coming, got hugs and kisses all around and some parting advice from Jim, Jeff and Gary. EL and Mary took a few extra moments and then it was off for some alone time.

CHAPTER 39

As we got to the door of the honeymoon suite, my feet froze to the ground. Tom opened the door but I couldn't move. I had so many conflicting emotions.

The first was my love for Tom and my duty to God. I have never loved anyone as much as I loved Tom. But I also felt like a traitor, winning his love for his seed. How could I honestly make love to him?

And then there was the nagging issue of how do I get his seed versus my faith in God. I know God had a plan but we were running out of time. My humanness was struggling with my faith.

Tom asked if I was alright and on the happiest day of my life, I started crying. Crying right there in the hallway in front of our honeymoon suite. For the first time in my life I truly felt lost. Just as I was sinking, these warm, loving arms were holding me close. The tighter I held on, the better I felt.

I think I cried in the hallway for 5 minutes and finally just sat down on the floor with my back to the wall. Tom sat next to me holding my hands. I remember him taking out his handkerchief and dabbing the tears from my face and he kept telling me it would be OK and that he loved me. Which is all I wanted to hear.

After I got some composure back, I told Tom that I was sorry. It had been a stressful day, that I loved him sooooo much and that I hadn't cried like that in many years. He was so gracious, just smiling and staring into my eyes. He later told me that when I was crying, the tears came out like diamonds and then flowed down my cheeks like a river full of sparkles.

I told him that I was OK and that I loved him and if he didn't hurry and get me into that room, we might be spending the night in the hallway. So up he jumped, gracefully pulled me to my feet and opened the door.

But again I was rooted to the floor. He gave me a look of deep concern but I smiled and said "well isn't it tradition for the groom to carry the bride across the threshold"?

This wave of relieve came over him and I was swept off my feet and into the room. Once the door closed, it didn't take either of us long to find the bed to complete what we had both been hoping for a long time.

As we crashed into each other's arms, the thought that kept going through my mind was "I have faith Lord! I have faith Lord! I have faith!"

In the middle of our love making, I was filled with the Holy Spirit and I knew that I could heal Tom. The Holy Spirit started flowing from me to him and I knew that his vasectomy was healed. But I couldn't stop it, I couldn't control it, I wanted this to last forever and I kept pouring the Holy Spirit into him. I could feel it flow down his legs and knew that he had a weak ACL which healed. I felt it flow up his chest and heal a broken rib and finally, I felt it flow into his brain and heal an aneurism.

I felt every nerve, every muscle and every heartbeat. I could live like this forever, with this connection to another human being but I needed to stop. I also realized that I couldn't just stop or Tom and I would implode. So gradually, slowly I pulled back.

Upon climax, I knew that I had Tom's seed. I knew I loved him more than I had ever loved anyone else. I knew that I had completed my mission. I knew I was in trouble. I knew the meaning of the Angel's warning.

CHAPTER 40

As we got to the door of the honeymoon suite, I opened the door and turned to let EL in. I couldn't read her face because it seemed like so many emotions were flowing through her. And it was like she was nailed to the ground.

I asked if she was alright and this river of tears started coming from her. My first thoughts were, Am I going to be jilted at the door of the honeymoon suite? Is she having second thoughts? Did I do something wrong? I hate it when girls cry. I never know what to do and I always do the wrong thing.

So I gave her a hug and told her I loved her. She hugged me back like it was going to be her last hug ever. And then she sat down on the carpet. Seriously, we are three feet from our room and she is crying in the hallway. So I sat down with her and held her hands, not knowing what else to do.

The river eventually slowed to a small creek and then stopped. She hugged me again and apologized for ruining the moment. We talked for a little bit and after a huge sigh, she said she was OK.

I got up and helped her to her feet. I opened the door again, turned to her hoping she was coming in only to find her planted in the ground again. My first thought was please don't start crying again. And then she said "well aren't you going to carry me across the threshold"? Relief and a big smile were my answers as I swept her off her feet.

It didn't take us long to get to the part I had been thinking about for many months. And it was everything I imagined and more. She was radiant, beautiful, sexy and cute. Wow!

I have never experienced anything like our love making that night. This energy seemed to be pulsing through me. It was like all my nerves were on hyper alert. It was like she was a part of me and me a part of her. It was like being in Heaven. To paraphrase 2 Corinthians, "*I was caught up to paradise and [felt] things so astounding that they cannot be expressed in words*". Over the years we would have incredible love making but nothing ever came close to that night.

When we were done, there was a feeling of withdrawal. It felt like energy was been pulled out of me. I was drained but in love. I might feel worn out but I wasn't about to let go.

I remember staying connected for a long time and not talking at all. Just being with her was enough.

CHAPTER 41

It was a fantastic time at the hotel. The most loving two days I had ever spent with anyone and now we were back at my apartment. We had to get everything packed and shipped to our new place. When we got right down to it, our everything wasn't that much and didn't even fill the two cars we would be driving to Washington DC.

I had been waiting to talk with Mary and she had been waiting for me. We finally got some time alone to catch up.

"How was it EL?"

"Mary, it was the most glorious two days I have ever spent with anyone. You and I have done some amazing things but they don't top the past two days with Tom."

"Did you get the seed?"

"Oh yes and we are in big trouble."

"How are we in trouble? What happened?"

"Remember my dream. Remember what the angel said?"

"Something about you being able to heal or something like that?"

"Exactly like that. I would have the power to heal but there would be long term consequences without restraint. And we have long term consequences."

"Explain please."

"So as we are making love, I am filled with the Holy Spirit. It starts to flow into Tom and I can sense it healing his vasectomy. But I couldn't stop. I continued to let the Holy Spirit flow. I knew it healed his ACL which would go bad in 5 years. I felt it heal the cracked rib that had never healed right. I felt it heal a brain aneurism that would have burst in less than a year and killed him. I let it flow until I could feel every nerve in his body. I had become one with him and he had become one with me. I could even tell when he lost a hair."

"And to top it all off, had I not been ready when he came, I would have passed out again. As it was, I saw stars and my eyes rolled in the back of my head. Finally, this happened almost every time we made love."

"Yeah. So."

"So. So!" I almost screamed. "He is going to live for a long time. He is almost perfect" I whispered.

"How long?"

"Like Methuselah long."

"Holy shit. We are in trouble. What do we do now?"

"You are the smart one. You tell me. I have been praying nonstop, except of course when I was otherwise distracted, for an answer. And nothing."

"You could just leave him EL."

"I can't leave him. How is he going to explain living to 200 years old? What is he going to do when all his friends are dead? And his second set of friends are dead. And his third set of friends. What is he going to do for money? We know how to reinvent ourselves only because we made a lot of mistakes along the way. We can't leave him to himself?"

"You're right EL. We can't abandon him."

"Oh Mary, Mary, Mary. What have I done? My love for Tom has gone too far. Sometimes when I think of it, I get sick to my stomach and almost throw up."

"Uh EL. The sick and throw up is from being pregnant. You always were a wimp."

"No. I'm not pregnant. I will carry the seed until Tom's death, remember."

And there was silence for a long time followed by Tom walking into the room.

CHAPTER 42

Mary and I didn't get any alone time the rest of the day. It was another passionate night, YES! It was also another sleepless night for me. After Tom fell asleep, I spent the rest of the night on my knees praying. Whenever Tom stirred, I would hurry back into bed until he settled down and then back on my knees again.

God was silent and I wept.

CHAPTER 43

I awoke in the morning wrapped in Tom's arms and I had a peace about us. I'm not sure when it came or why it came but I had a peace.

Tom had to run some errands in the morning which gave Mary and me some time alone. I told her about my evening and she shared that she had also been on her knees most of the night. She also shared that there was peace in her heart. At that, I almost leaped across the table and gave her a bear hug. We both smiled, giggled and then got lost in thought.

It was then that Mary asked what I had shared with Tom about our upbringing. I filled her in on what I said including the Healing Tree. At the mention of the Healing Tree, she had this look like she had just had an epiphany.

"EL. I still have two pieces of the dried fruit from the Healing Tree. I have been carrying it around for all this time not understanding why. Now I know."

"I'm not following Mary."

"What if we get Tom to eat the dried fruit? In future years, you could say that it was the eating of the fruit which is extending his life. It would also explain why you and I are not getting older also."

"Do we really want to do this Mary? Isn't that lying to him?"

"Not really. If we had shared the fruit with him before you healed him, it would have had some of the same effect. It may not have been as extensive but it would have done some healing. It is the best I can think of and it explains why I have been carrying it around forever."

"Wow, EL said. "That is some serious thinking but I'm not sure. I think we need to pray on it tonight."

"We can't wait too long because you two are leaving in two days and I'm flying back to London. I can offer it as a wedding present?"

"Yeah. That could work. But I still think we need to pray on it. OK?"

"OK EL. One more day won't hurt. We have a lot of them" she said with a smile.

We hugged and started talking about other things just as Tom got home. He had stopped at the store on the way back and picked up food for a big American breakfast. He was going to make bacon, omelets with tomato, mushrooms, spinach and cheese along with buttermilk pancakes.

The three of us hadn't realized how hungry we were until we started to clean up and there wasn't anything left. We all just laughed.

I gave Tom the option of cleaning up the kitchen or helping me pack up the bedroom. He wished Mary and me good luck and started to clean the table.

CHAPTER 44

About 4:00 o'clock, Mary declared that she was hungry and would buy if we would take her out dancing. That sounded good to EL and me so we gladly accepted her offer. Mary headed off to the guest bedroom while EL and I headed to our room.

We jumped into the shower and had it not been for Mary, we probably wouldn't have made it out of the apartment. EL worked hard to keep us separated and it worked some of the time. After the shower, we heard a knock on the door with Mary asking EL if she could borrow something to wear.

EL picked out some clothes for me to wear and sent me packing. The girls were going to get to looking pretty and I was in the way.

I left the room with a pouty face which only made Mary and EL laugh.

About 30 minutes later, just when I figured they had fallen in, they both emerged from the bedroom. EL was in the red dress she wore the night of our first date and Mary was in something I hadn't seen EL wear before but was just as stunning. My mouth was gaping open and both ladies came up to me, put their fingers under my chin, pushed it up, gave me a kiss on the cheek at the same time and both whispered "Thank you" in unison.

It was scary how much they looked alike, how beautiful they were and how similar in mannerism they were. That same thought ran through my head about some poor bloke running into them at a bar when they dressed alike and getting totally confused. They would just run over top of him. P.S. bloke is a new word that Mary taught me while she was here so I tried to use it once.

Mary wanted to go back to the Blue Moon East, which totally broke my heart, not. I called ahead to let the owner know we were coming and he reserved a table for the three of us. He asked how our marriage was going and what we were doing next. We shared that this would be our last time for dinner in some time since we were leaving for Washington DC in two days.

He and his wife made a big deal about our dinner. We didn't want for anything and when it was time to leave, there were tears in our eyes and theirs. Even though we hadn't known them long, we had all come to enjoy each other. Over the years to come, EL and I would come back to the Blue Moon East every year for our anniversary. We celebrated the birth of their grandchildren and attended their funerals.

Dancing that evening was so much fun. EL and Mary decided to pick on a 'cute' guy that Mary wanted to get to know better. They messed with his mind for about two hours before they fessed up and both showed up together. He was a little irritated until Mary whispered something in his ear and they disappeared. That was our cue to head home also as we had a busy day coming up to finish the packing.

CHAPTER 45

Mary and I agreed that giving the fruit to Tom was the best idea. We had both prayed on it and having not heard anything from God, decided to move forward with the plan.

After dinner, Mary went up to Tom with this really neat package. She had gone somewhere to get a box and some really nice wrapping paper. I had never seen anything like it.

"Tom and EL, I have been thinking about what to give you two for your wedding. Tom, if you would do the honor of opening the box."

I watched as he opened it and saw two dried pieces of fruit and that he wasn't impressed. But that didn't stop Mary.

"EL shared that on our farm, grandfather had a tree called the Healing Tree. When we left the farm, he gave each of us a parting gift. I don't remember what EL's gift was but mine was some of the fruit from the Healing Tree that he dried and sealed for later use. He said that I would know when the right time to use it was. As my gift to you and EL, I would like each of you to have one of my last two pieces so you may have a long and healthy life together."

Tom was so impressed by the gift and the thought that Mary had put into her gift, that a tear ran down his cheek. He stood and gave Mary one of his bear hugs with a huge grin on his face. When he finally put Mary down, she melted into one of the chairs. Afterwards, she told me that she could feel the love pouring into her like she had never felt before.

Tom was in a funny mood and wanted us to feed each other like newlyweds normally do with the cake. We hadn't had a cake so I agreed. It was so simple but so touching.

Afterwards, we opened a bottle of wine to celebrate that we were done packing, new beginnings and new family. Tom headed to bed around 10:00 while Mary and I stayed up talking well into the night.

PART 2

CHAPTER 46

EL and I settled into our routine in Washington DC. I was working for a think tank. We worked with government agencies on creating policy that worked with some large businesses helping them interact with the government. We also consulted with the military on a broad range of topics, which is where I was assigned. It was both fascinating and mundane at the same time.

The fascinating side was being able to help create direction. We were talking about weapons systems that wouldn't be deployed for years and what needed to be invented to make them a reality. On the mundane side, interacting with our government can be very repetitive. At times, it would seem like I would visit ten to fifteen congressmen and get asked the same question by their staff and then by them. Having to answer one question thirty times got old but that is how things get done, mostly.

EL was working for an archeology company out of Israel. She was doing historical research, spending most of her time in the Library of Congress and other libraries with, as she would say, "old, dusty manuscripts." She loved it and she was good at it. She hadn't shared with me while we were dating but she was fluent in five languages and could read a few more.

She was looking for the clues that would lead an archeologist to new finds. We have all heard at least one story about the piece of paper that was stuck at the back of a book which pointed to untold riches and fame. She was looking for that piece of paper.

One day she came home very excited. She had found a tidbit on Joan of Arc in a manuscript from the Oxford University Library. I was asking her why it was important and she was doing her best to explain. I listened intently but still didn't get the significance. She said with this information, she could imagine three different stories about Joan of Arc's family history that were previously unknown. If she could find one or two more pieces of information, she would be able to narrow that down.

I asked her to share one of her stories and that became our family tradition. When each of us would find something new or share something of significance, we had to create a tale to go with the information. For me it was always conjecture. As I will learn years later, for EL it is was true history.

CHAPTER 47

Double nickel, 55, is a great reason to party. Being promoted to COO three weeks before your 55th birthday is a reason to amp up the party to a new level.

When EL started planning my birthday party, she envisioned a small gathering at our row house. But with the promotion, she thought it would be a great reason to go all out. She was even having Mary come in from somewhere.

Over the years we had found another little Chinese restaurant similar to the Blue Moon East which we would frequent at least once a month. EL had gotten to know the owner's wife and specifically began to learn the Chinese language so she could communicate with them. This fascinated the wife that someone would care enough to learn the language just to be able to talk with her. But that was EL. So when it was time to move the party outside of our row house, the restaurant was the logical place. EL made arrangements for 50 of us to take over the restaurant beginning at 5:00 pm on Sunday.

As you would expect, the food was to die for, the drinks were stronger than normal and everyone had fun. I received some nice presents including two bottles of priceless wine, a bottle of Liquor 43, my favorite sipping spirits and untold cards making fun of my age and sexual prowess. All was taken in the manner in which it was intended.

All the cards were addressed to "The Kid". This was the nickname I had at the office. Even though I was now 55, I still looked like I was in my early 30's. I found this to be both a blessing and a curse. On the blessing side, I was underestimated most of the times by my adversaries and ended up kicking their asses. But that only happened once before they each learned.

One the curse side, there were many times my input was dismissed because the Congressman or Senator or their staff thought they were dealing with some young whipper snapper. I learned to bring along one of the older looking folks in our group to meetings with people like this to provide the appropriate ambiance.

As the evening wound down, the last person to leave was my mentor, friend and boss. When I first joined the firm, he saw something in me and has been the guiding force behind my rise to the number two position. As he was leaving he said "great party Tom. You will have to find a way to top it next year when I announce my retirement and promote you to CEO. Oh, and take tomorrow off to spend time with your wife and her sister." So with a wink, a smile and a handshake, he was out the door knowing he had just left an IED in my lap.

Mary, EL and I packed up the presents and cards, thanked the owners, gave them a big tip and headed home. I shared with them what my boss said and Mary and EL were excited to spend Monday with me. They had already made plans for the day to visit the White House and invited me along.

CHAPTER 48

The day with Mary and EL brought about some interesting conversations. We headed to the White House for our tour around noon. The President was out of town so we didn't get to meet him. I had briefed him once and knew some of the staffers from my work so after the official tour, we got to go "behind the scenes". It was fun to be able to show off.

It was during the behind the scenes tour that our first conversation happened. The staffer I worked with most was able to let us peek into the Oval Office and while there, the Vice President wondered by. We were introduced and she remarked about how young we looked and I couldn't be the driving force behind my company that she had heard of. The staffer then spoke up and said that my nickname was The Kid. The Vice President agreed wholeheartedly and remarked that she now knew why everyone underestimated me. I took it as a compliment.

We stopped after the tour in one of the trendy restaurants in Georgetown for a glass of wine and to enjoy the day. We got carded, which wasn't unusual, and when the young girl delivered the wine, she commented that we were the youngest looking 55 year olds she had ever seen and hoped she looked that good when she was our age. She asked what our secret was. I kidded with her that it was true love, good exercise and great sex, to which she blushed. EL just smiled and gave me one of her kisses on the cheek.

Our final stop was at one of the regular restaurants EL and I enjoyed going to that we wanted to take Mary to. Our regular waiter was off and the owner asked if it was OK for us to have one of the new girls. We tried to be gracious so we said yes and this bubbly, collage age girl headed our way. I like to engage with our waiters so I started a banter with her. She did a good job, got our orders right, showed up at the appropriate times and the bill was as it should be. After dinner, the owner stopped back over to get our impression and shared a comment the waitress had said to him. She had remarked how young we were to him and when he told her our approximate age, she was shocked. He shared the comment as a compliment but it got me thinking. When something happens to me three times in one day, I take notice.

When we got home, I brought up the subject to EL and Mary. A look passed between them that I couldn't figure out, you know that look of something only the two of them know. A look I had seen a few times before. The two of them hemmed and hawed and eventually changed the subject before I could get anything solid from them.

When we went to bed, I brought it up to EL again. She could see that it was bothering me and promised to talk some with Mary the next day and give me their thoughts at dinner. This and a kiss from EL placated me and I was asleep in no time.

CHAPTER 49

When I got home from work on Tuesday, the house was a variable potpourri of smells. EL and Mary had made lasagna so there was this smell of pasta and pasta sauce. They had garlic bread warming in the oven which blended so well with the lasagna. And earlier in the day, they had made a fresh apple pie so there was this lingering smell of apples and cinnamon. From a senses perspective, they had hit a home run.

I also made what had become a normal mistake which the girls always laughed about. I came into the kitchen and spun EL around and gave her a huge welcome home kiss. Upon disentangling myself from EL, Mary confessed that it was really her. And looking over my shoulder, I saw the real EL smiling her smile which always seemed to say "we gotcha again". She got a big kiss also and all was right with the world.

Over dinner, we started talking about aging or the lack thereof. Mary and EL shared that they had spent a lot of time thinking about it when it dawned on Mary what had been her wedding gift to us. She talked about how her grandfather would give the fruit to those in need with the warning that it would heal them but may have a side effect. When pressed by the person receiving the gift on what the side effect could be, she said that grandfather usually said that it was different for each person.

Mary's theory was that since EL and I had eaten the fruit when we were not sick, it could have worked its healing powers into an already healthy person and made us healthier. This would explain why both of us seemed to be in our early 30's when in fact we were at least 55. I started doing the calculations in my head and said that at this pace, we could live to be 150 to 200 years old.

All of a sudden, I was a little scared and by looking at EL and Mary, they seemed to share my concern. The questions that started running through my mind and that I began blurting out where, how do we afford to be in retirement for 100 years? How do we explain this to who knows who? I don't want to be a lab rat where I get poked and prodded for 50 years. There were a whole bunch of other questions but hopefully you see the breadth of my reality.

EL and Mary started talking through some scenarios and Mary shared that she had eaten some of the fruit also so she may be in the same circumstances. After not making much progress, we tabled the discussion for another day, promising to make it our dinner talk the following day.

I got a little depressed with the discussion and ended up hitting the wine a little hard. It was the first time in 25 years that I went to bed a little drunk, though I was told by EL the next day when I complained about a headache that I was a lot drunk. I promised myself to keep a clearer head going forward.

After I left for work, EL and Mary started reviewing how the conversation had gone with me the previous night. They were happy that I had bought into their story but sad they couldn't share the real truth. They both looked at each other and said they hoped they could keep this up for the next 100 years.

CHAPTER 50

I spent the day totally distracted. I couldn't stop thinking about living to 150 years old. At times I would get depressed thinking that everyone I knew would pass away before me. How many funerals would I need to go to? When would people start noticing that I was the only one left? How many wars would I have to see with their wasted deaths?

At other times I would think of the endless possibilities. With an active mind and such a long history, I could be one of the kings of industry. Who would be able to stop me? I also thought of all the inventions that would be invented. What new technologies would I see? Would there be medical breakthroughs that would add even more years to my life?

My secretary worked really hard to keep me on track. I was late for three internal meetings and was barely on time for a meeting with one of the Senators. Each time I used the excuse of being a little hung over from my birthday party and spending too much time thinking about how old I was. People bought that excuse but I realized that I was going to have to get my head back into the game again tomorrow.

I called EL about 3:00 pm and gave her a quick overview of the day. She reassured me that we could spend more time talking about it over dinner, with no wine. I don't know how she does it but knowing she cared and would be there was all I needed. I finished the day strong.

CHAPTER 51

When I got home, EL and Mary were there to greet me. EL shared that she and Mary had spent a good portion of the day talking about our predicament and had some thoughts.

The first thought was that we couldn't stay where we were for 150 years. They didn't have a plan, though I thought I saw a look go back and forth between them a few times. They felt we would have to pick an age to work to and then "retire to Florida or Arizona". Once we got to our destination, we could reinvent ourselves. This seemed logical, though jettisoning lifelong friends would be hard.

They also said that we would need to start figuring out what to do with our money. Did we want to start converting some of it to cash, move it off-shore, invest in gold or leave it in the bank. A hundred year retirement is a long time to plan for.

We also talked about the option of not retiring. How could we reinvent ourselves as younger versions of who we were, get jobs and work within an organization without running across former colleagues? This was going to be the hardest thing to do unless we moved into totally new fields where there would be minimal overlap. We decided that this was going to take a lot more thinking and since we weren't in a big rush, we figured we would decide this later.

We circled back around to retirement. At my firm, it was pretty standard to retire at 65 so we decided that I would follow tradition. EL said that the folks in her line of work sometimes worked until they were ready to pass away so she could continue doing her work or leave it at any time. I could see that she said that with a heavy heart because this was something she had come to love. Reading old tomes and trying to discern their meaning was fun for her and she was really good at it. In our years since college, she had been credited with one major find and assisted on a half dozen more that she was willing to admit to.

We next turned to Mary to see what she was thinking. She said that she flitter bitted about the world as it was and didn't really stay in any one place more that 3-5 years. She hadn't gotten married or stayed with anyone for longer than a year so she felt she could continue to morph into a new person. It was funny that in that moment, I saw a sadness in her eyes when she told us this and my heart went out to her.

With a high level plan in place, dinner consumed, the dishes done and no wine drunk, I realized it was late and I had a big day coming up. I kissed the girls goodnight, headed to bed and left them to talk.

Once I was gone and some time had passed, EL asked Mary "how do you think it went? Do you think he bought into it? It seemed like it to me."

Mary replied "I think he believes us. I know he loves you very much and values your thoughts. We just need to make sure that we don't mess this up. It could be a long, lonely life for him if we do."

CHAPTER 52

Over the next 10 years, EL and I worked to maximize our portfolio while at the same time moving it to places that weren't as strict as the United States. We created multiple accounts in Switzerland and the Cayman Islands. We also set up accounts in Ireland, Israel and Australia, all places that EL traveled to as part of her research. Diversity is important in a portfolio so we decided diversity was important in our banking also.

Mary was also busy spreading her wealth around. She chose London, the Bahamas, India and Turkey which I thought was an odd choice. She said that it was at the heart of the troubles between religions so if we ever had to head to the Middle East, we would have a local presence. I couldn't fault her logic though I never pictured myself going there.

As 65 got closer, our friends began to ask what we were going to do. EL and I had decided that doing missionary work in sub-Saharan Africa or a remote part of Mongolia would be a good way for us to separate from our friends without them being able to check up on us. We could send notes and cards over the years, gradually cutting back communication until we were off the grid.

We had pretty much settled on Africa until one of our casual friends from church mentioned they were going there for a short term mission trip. Even though they would be going to a different country, we didn't want anyone "being close" so Mongolia it became.

My retirement party was over the top. When my administrative assistant, who had been with me for almost 30 years, started the planning process, it was her plan to have a small gathering. But once the word got out, the folks who I had worked with in both the government and industry wanted to attend. I hadn't realized how many people I had touched over the years and the final count on number of attendees was just short of 275 people. Grace and I kept trying to cut down on the number but I could tell a story or two about each of these folks.

We rented out a ballroom at one of the hotels and reserved a block of rooms. Before we knew it, the hotel was sold out for the weekend and the party expanded. Unofficial activities began on Friday evening and ran through to Monday breakfast when the last of the guests flew home. I was exhausted and EL just smiled the entire weekend. It was a great way to end the first part of our life.

CHAPTER 53

Six months later, we had sold all of our Earthly possessions except for the clothes we would be taking to Mongolia. Our world had gone from a beautiful four bedroom row house filled with antiques that EL had found around the world to three suitcases each.

EL had worked hard to find new homes for her precious pieces. She worked with dealers across the globe to get top dollar for most of the pieces. But four pieces in particular were never sold. One of them was a rare Ming vase that went to the son of the owners of Blue Moon East. We had continued to stay in touch with them, even investing in their expansion to five restaurants.

Another piece went to the Smithsonian. It was a rare Bible that EL had acquired in Ireland. She had come across it at an auction of an old abbey and had picked it up for a song. Once she got it back home, she realized that it was a priceless manuscript. We had a special case created for it that was sealed to keep the atmosphere out and had enjoyed it for years but it was now time to share it with the world.

The third piece went to our church. It was a picture of Christ that EL had purchased on one of her trips. Our pastor had been to our house many times and always commented on how beautiful the painting was. He said he always felt like he was in the presence of the Lord when he looked upon it. We felt that if it inspired him, it could also inspire others. The painting ended up in the Prayer Chapel and through the years, we were told it touched many a person.

The final piece or pieces was our dining room set including the hutch. Over the almost 30 years that my administrative assistant had worked for me, she and her family had been to our house many, many times. When EL found the dining room set and it first appeared at our house, Grace had commented on its exquisite beauty. Whenever she visited after that, she would always gravitate to the dining room to spend her time. When we told her that it would be coming to her house, tears just streamed down her cheeks. I think she cried for most of the evening.

So with everything gone and the row house sold, it was off to Mongolia.

CHAPTER 54

We successfully made it to one of the small villages in the remote Lake Uvs area. Our village had never seen an outsider and were surprised when the pretty redhead could speak their language after only a few days. I'm not sure if I shared this, but one of EL's strengths was languages. She could walk into any village on the planet and within a week she would be able to talk with them in their own language. I'm not bad at language but EL is a superstar.

We had been there about 3 months when we came across the first signs of Spring. With the weather turning warm, the locals recommended that we hike out to some of the small mountain lakes to get a better sense of our surroundings. They did warn that it could turn cold and dangerous in the mountains in a heartbeat so they encouraged us to pack for a week even though we were only going to be gone for two nights.

The locals were right. The mountain lakes were beautiful in the spring. The wildlife was everywhere, chirping at us from sun up to sundown for disturbing their space. We poked our feet into one of the lakes and that was all. It had to still be 32 degrees Fahrenheit.

We woke up the second day to some serious rumblings from deep within the mountain. We completed packing up and decided to head back to the village. As we reached the first lake, the mountain exploded below us and shook for what seemed like hours. When we recovered our senses, we realized that we had just experienced a major earthquake in an area that doesn't normally get them.

EL and I started rushing back to the village. We pushed hard for about 4 hours. As we came within view of the village we both stopped in shock. There was nothing left. I had never seen destruction on this scale before. All EL and I could do was hold each other and pray. I think we just sat there for at least an hour. As the shock began to wear off and the tears stopped flowing, we ventured closer only to find nothing. Later, the press would describe the destruction similar to the earthquake of 2015 in Nepal.

Sundown was coming quickly and we needed to make a plan to survive. We scavenged the village and found some usable food that we added to our stockpile from camping. We were also able to find our strongbox with our personal items including our passports. As the sun began to set, we had enough foodstuff to make it two weeks eating sparingly and hoping to find berries and other items in the woods. Our plan was to call for help using our SAT phone and touch base with Mary.

EL finally reached Mary after a few calls, waking her up again. EL gave her the short version of our situation and our plan. I didn't hear much of Mary's side of the conversation but I heard her when she screamed at EL to not call the authorities. I was pissed at Mary, thinking that she wanted us to die here in the middle of nowhere until EL calmed me down explaining Mary's plan.

We had always thought to use Mongolia as a place where we could fade away from our friends and then start a new life after 3-5 years. Mary explained the earthquake gave us the opportunity to move this timetable up. Before coming to Mongolia, we had created second identities that we would assume, including passports. Since we had the passports with us, Mary was suggesting we execute the plan now.

There was a minor city about a week's hike away where we could blend in. It was unaffected by the earthquake and would become a staging area for some of the rescue activities so a few extra young Americans wouldn't be out of place. It was a stroke of genius and the hand of God working to move our plan along.

Mary suggested that we power off all our electronics because we had to have them last about a week. We would check in with her once a day giving her our GPS location and she would chart our course making daily corrections. She also said that if we came across any of the rescue teams before getting to the city, that we should do our best to be invisible. There would be too many questions. Mary would also begin the process of inquiries about us to build the backstory of our death.

After hanging up from Mary, EL and I decided we didn't want to spend the night in the village. We packed up our supplies and head down what was left of the road, getting an hour outside of the village to one of the lakes where we spent our first night.

The hike would take us nine hard days. On three different occasions, we had to move off the road and stay hidden as rescue teams were heading into the area. Each night, EL and Mary would talk. We would give her a quick update and she would keep us posted on local updates. The next to last night, our SAT phone battery died so we continued on alone.

Upon reaching the city, we found a small café where we could recharge the SAT phone. The coffee was both terrible and wonderful at the same time and the local pastry was the best I had ever had. Mary was doing the happy dance when she finally heard from us. She had booked a room for us in one of the local hotels, explaining to the owner that we had been hiking, heard about the earthquake and were coming to help. With directions to the hotel, EL and I left the coffee shop and headed to the hotel.

When we got to the hotel the owner came out to greet us, trying to speak the few words of English he knew. EL pretended to know some of the local language so between the two of them, we were welcomed and given one of the nicer rooms. The owner asked us to dine with him that evening and he would introduce us the next day to the head of the local rescue efforts.

When we got to the room, we found the shower was warm, the bed was soft and the room was clean. After almost two weeks camping, it was more than we hoped for. We took a shower and a short nap before heading down to dinner.

Today was the first day of our new life. We would be known to the outside world as Melba and Tomas. We chose these names so if we slipped into calling each other EL and Tom, it wouldn't be unusual.

CHAPTER 55

We headed down to dinner with the following plan. We would communicate in English even though we were now fluent in the local dialect. We would slowly "learn" their dialect over the next month or so up to a beginner's level of knowledge. We felt this was the best tactic. This would also allow us to gather intelligence by listening to their conversations. So with a plan in place, we headed down to dinner with our host.

The hotel owner was an interesting character. One of Mongolia's newly minted entrepreneurs, Alex as he liked to be called, was all about business. He dressed the part of a successful Western businessman and liked to show off his success and influence. Throughout the night, Alex took the time to introduce us to everyone that walked past our table. It seems we were one of the first English speaking recovery workers to arrive so it was a major coup for him to be able to introduce us as his friend staying at his hotel. If we thought we were going to be anonymous, we were mistaken.

One of the last people to stop over was Li Qiang, the head of the recovery effort for the area. He was an Oxford trained engineer who could speak English quite well. We made more progress with him in 10 minutes than the whole time we had spent with Alex. We were asked to come to his office the next day to see how we could help. His most pressing needs were around logistics and communication. We said we could help in both areas though we cautioned about our lack of being able to speak with the locals. He wasn't too concerned with that saying he had plenty of people he could pair up with us.

By the end of the evening, we were exhausted but happy. Alex's cook was over the top good. When we showed interest in the local dishes he began to bring out sampler plates of everything. Some of the food we had no any idea what it was but it was all good, most great and some exceptional. We asked Alex if would could get a tour of the kitchen in front of the cook which sent him off smiling from ear to ear. Alex promised us a tour but said they would need to make the kitchen spotless to show to Americans.

After almost four hours, we headed back up to our room. When we got to the room, we noticed that our stuff had been moved just slightly. Many years in the government intelligence industry had made me observant of my surroundings. I gave EL a big kiss and hug to hide my telling her of my suspicions and to be careful what we said. EL headed into the bathroom to clean up with the water running while I was in charge of reconnaissance.

The first thing I did was just sit and relax on the bed. I noticed a hidden camera on the nightstand which I was able to cover up with my shirt as I got undressed. I then found two additional listening devices in the room. With the recon done, I headed into the bathroom to get ready for bed. I found a third listening device on the side of the toilet. We were going to have to be real careful and we were going to have to leave quickly.

We whispered about whether to have sex or not. In the end, we acted like we were too exhausted. We hope we fooled our hosts.

CHAPTER 56

The next day at the Ministry Office was interesting. I noticed leaving the hotel that we had a tail on us. They followed discreetly but not to the trained eye. Once at the Ministry Office, we were brought in to see Li Qiang. Our discussion with him lasted almost two hours ranging from our personal background, to why we were really there and to our family. Twice we were interrupted by other workers who came into the office in a panic to talk about an urgent matter. It was obvious that they were trying to see if we really understood the local language by watching our body language. Fortunately, we had talked about this on the way over and I think we passed their tests.

Finally, he asked if we would help with crafting messages to the world on the local conditions. This was something that we could do though we would need to work with a translator to make sure our message was consistent with what they wanted to get out. He introduced us to Minmin and she became our constant companion.

With Day One half over, Minmin took us to lunch at her favorite restaurant. We came to find out that Minmin had grown up in the area and had been fortunate enough to attend University in Beijing. After her studies were complete, she came back home to work for Li Qiang, her uncle. She was very excited to be assigned to us because she would be able to work on her English.

Minmin and EL spent most of the meal talking about little things while my mind reviewed the morning meeting. I wanted to make sure that we hadn't slipped anywhere during the cross examination. My final analysis is that we got an A- grade and would need to continue to improve.

In the afternoon, we worked with Minmin to draft a three paragraph announcement to the world. It was a tough process. Minmin would do her best to explain to EL what she wanted conveyed in the announcement. EL would write the words in English and then review them with Minmin. She would then take the paragraphs out of the room for review and return with recommended changes or questions about specific definitions of words.

During each time out of the office, we were left alone to talk. Knowing that we were being watched and recorded, EL and I talked about our time hiking in the woods, about getting back home to visit with our families and how exciting it was going to be to talk about helping. Each time Minmin came back, she had a hidden smile like she had approved of what we had talked about. It was serious business but EL and I made a game of it.

We wrapped up the day with approval from the Ministry Office on the three paragraph announcement. Minmin offered to walk home with us but we convinced her to drop us off at a local place to buy a cup of coffee where we could watch the traffic and relax. She took us to a quaint shop just off the beaten path, talked with the owner to get us what we wanted and after making sure we knew how to get back to the hotel went on her way.

EL and I enjoyed our coffee and our time alone. I could see that we were still being watched so we assumed we were being listened in on. It was scary but fun living our own spy novel.

CHAPTER 57

We were midway through our third week when I began to notice some subtle changes. I'm not sure if it was the large infusion of Westerners and others coming to help or if it was something about us. Reacting on the conservative side, EL and I decided to send Mary our extraction emergency word of SNOW. This would trigger Mary to come up with some excuse for us to leave.

We had picked the word SNOW because it was the middle of the summer and there was none to been seen anywhere. We knew the area received a considerable amount of snow during the winter months and hopefully this would allow us a way to work it in.

EL was brilliant that afternoon in talking with Minmin. She started asking questions about the climate and what it was like during the rest of the year. Was it always so hot? How long were the winter nights? Did they get a lot of rain in the spring? By asking questions about each season, EL was able to mask the conversation we would have with Mary later that evening.

We had gotten in the habit of calling Mary every third day. With today being our scheduled day to call and EL having been recorded talking about the climate with Minmin off and on throughout the day, we felt comfortable with using our emergency word.

During the call, EL shared what she learned about the climate, telling her how fascinating it was. EL talked about the rains in the spring and the snow amounts the area could expect in winter. She also told Mary about Minmin's thoughts on how beautiful fall was in the area. We knew that Mary received our message when she asked back if they got any tornadoes like we had experienced while living in Kansas. With the call completed, we just needed to survive until we received the "emergency" call from Mary.

Two days later, we received a call from Mary at about 11:17 am. We were in a meeting with Minmin working on another announcement. Mary's first call was ignored by EL along with the second one. When she called a third time in a row, Minmin made EL answer it. That is when we found out that EL and Mary's mom had suffered a stroke and was in intensive care. Mary shared that they didn't know how long their mom was going to last and it was recommended that everyone get there as soon as possible to say their goodbyes.

EL broke down on the phone and thanked Mary. When she hung up, she shared with Minmin and me what Mary had told her and just started bawling. She even got Minmin crying. Minmin comforted EL and then left to make arrangements for us to leave. With the help of the minister, we were on a military transport that evening to Beijing to catch an international flight home. Two days later, we were in London with Mary. And as a side note, our first evening together without being watched and listened to was most excellent. I don't remember getting a whole lot of sleep.

CHAPTER 58

We spent the next month casually planning the next phase of our life. We stayed with Mary in London in her one bedroom apartment. By day, the three of us were the typical American tourists. I had never been to London, so the tourist gig was fun. EL had been here quite a bit and really wanted to show me what she used to do but we were constrained because she was supposed to have been killed in Mongolia. We knew the word had gotten out because one of her old colleagues in DC had forwarded to Mary a sympathy card they had received from one of the museums EL had frequented in London.

London is a big city and we had plenty to see. We had a scare in week four when we were out. EL and I had ditched into a coffee shop to get some biscuits and coffee. Mary decided to stay outside and enjoy the morning rush. While standing there, one of EL's old colleagues started talking to Mary thinking she was EL. When Mary explained that EL had been her twin sister, the woman started crying and apologizing to Mary. She talked with Mary for 15 minutes or so about how much she loved EL. Coming out of the coffee shop, we almost walked right into the conversation only seeing the danger about three steps away. We had to pretend to not know Mary and continue down the road, around the corner and back to the apartment where Mary finally caught up to us.

This convinced us that London was not going to be a good place for phase two. It was time to get serious. We also knew that we needed to limit our sightseeing. I was disappointed but understood.

We decided to create a game out of our planning process and base it on the video game "Where in the World is Carmen Sandiego?" We called our game, Where in the World should EL and Tom Hide?

Here are the facts we created for our new life. We would both be 25 years old, which was totally feasible based upon our looks. We would be two people who were self-taught geniuses who liked to live off the grid. We had met during the years that our parents had done home based education and would get together with other families who were also doing home based education. When we were both 21 years old, we decided to visit places around the world and stay there until we wanted to move on.

We decided that in the past four years, we had lived in Washington D.C., London and Mongolia. Since we could tell stories of each town, we felt comfortable with this back story. We also could talk about some of the short trips we had taken to various places like Istanbul and Tel Aviv where Mary had done significant research. Coming from families of wealth, we had the means to afford our lifestyle.

We talked about many different places to move to but two of them kept coming to the forefront, South Africa and Australia. EL and I had never visited either of these countries so we felt there would be minimal opportunity to run into someone we knew. Both countries were far from our old stomping grounds and none of our old friends had ever talked about visiting either country. Both countries spoke some form of English so we wouldn't have to struggle with a language barrier. And finally, both were big enough that we could blend into the countryside if an emergency situation arose.

So how do you decide when everything is even? You flip a coin!

South Africa was the winner so we began our plans for life south of the equator.

CHAPTER 59

When we started looking for jobs, one of the criteria for the companies we targeted was that they were not international companies or did work for the government. We didn't want to be put in a position where we could run into someone we worked with in our previous life.

I got hired by a food processing company as a management trainee. It was a family run business that realized they needed to continue to build and create leaders within the company. I hit it off with the patriarch during my first interview. He was a bit of a buff on bicycling and a big fan of the Tour de France. Upon seeing some of his pictures, I shared that EL and I had spent three weeks following the Tour around France. The interview lasted for 90 minutes and we spent about 60 of those minutes talking bicycles.

EL found a job at the University of Cape Town as a research assistant. The University has a rich history of research in many areas and EL was fortunate to get hired into the Department of Archaeology. This was going to be right up her alley though she would have to be careful to not be too knowledgeable.

We were in South Africa for about five months when the troubles in the Middle East exploded. We had already been through the Arab Spring, the war in Syria and the rise of more terrorist groups but hadn't seen anything like this.

It was confirmed that Iran had created a nuclear bomb so Israel attacked. The United States came to the support of Israel as did some of their allies in the Middle East. And this quickly escalated into a religious war.

EL and Mary did a lot of talking on the phone. They also did a lot of praying. EL shared with me some of her revelations from her prayers. Ideas like: this is what the Father wants and this is the beginning of the End Times. She was never specific but I could see the deep belief in her.

I would ask what we should be doing and she would say all that needs to be done is done. Sometimes she would begin to cry and there was nothing I could do to console her. She would just mumble, it is all my fault. I didn't know what to do so I just held her.

After some of her crying, she would just want to be alone. I would peek in on her and she would be kneeling in silence in prayer.

CHAPTER 60

South Africa wasn't directly affected by the wars in the Middle East but we felt the economic effects. Trade to that area was almost stopped. Trade to the United States and Europe was slowed by about 25 percent. The only trading area that wasn't really affected was Asia Pacific.

Neither of our jobs were in jeopardy of being interrupted in the short term. Food still needed to be processed and the research at the University continued. At my job, I was making good progress in the trainee program and was trying to not show too much knowledge.

We were installing some new equipment similar to what one of my former clients had installed five years earlier. I pretty much knew how it should be installed and our team was making a critical mistake. I kept trying to subtly get my point across but no one was listening to the new kid. On the day where we were at the point of no return, I finally became very forceful about the problem and got fired.

But instead of leaving, I went to the owner's office. I explained the problem to him and he was skeptical at best. How would I know better than his chief engineer? I explained that I was big into reading instructions and that I had poured over what we had received and believed I was right. My request of him was to stop for the day and call the manufacturer. If I was wrong, I would be gone. If I was right, I was saving him a lot of money because on the path they were going, the piece of equipment would be ruined.

I explained to him where I believed the problem was. I sketched out how they were doing the installation and how I thought it should be installed.

He asked me to wait outside while he brought his chief engineer in. They had a long conversation and I didn't make a new friend that day. After their conversation, the owner and the chief engineer were off to the plant with my drawings, smart phone in hand and the manufacturer on the line.

It was a long wait. My ass was flat and my patience was near the end when the owner returned and asked me into his office. I had been right and the chief engineer hadn't been happy. From what the owner shared, the chief engineered had still wanted to do it his way even after the manufacture had said he was wrong. In fact, as I was to learn later, it had escalated into a full scale shouting match between the chief engineer and the owner.

After the owner told me the story, we sat silently for what seemed like forever. One thing I had learned over the course of my life was, there are times when you need to be silent and let the other person speak first. And this was one of those times.

Finally, the owner seemed to come to a decision. He again asked me to wait as he walked out of the office. About 30 minutes later, he returned and shared that he had just let the chief engineer go. Again, we sat in silence while he was making another major decision which totally caught me off guard. He asked me to become the new chief engineer. I protested saying I was new, I was inexperienced and there were more senior people who should get the job. He explained back that all my reasons were valid but I was the only one with the nerve to come see him and do what was right. That was more important to him than anything else.

So in the midst of turmoil in the world, I had just created turmoil at work. I was sure that there would be pushback from three specific folks and shared my thoughts with the owner. He said he would make sure that my back was covered.

The next day, the owner called a companywide meeting. He talked about yesterday's events to everyone and how we almost made a multi-million dollar mistake. But for the courage of one person who believed he was right, the mistake was averted. He announced me as the new chief engineer. He also made it very clear that if anyone was opposed to his announcement that they were free to leave and a generous separation agreement would be given. He also make it abundantly clear that if people chose to stay, they had better be onboard with this new arrangement because there would be no tolerance for discussion and no generous offer forthcoming.

Not surprisingly, two of the three folks who I had thought would be a problem took the separation agreement. The third person became my most trusted lieutenant.

CHAPTER 61

EL was making progress in her job also. She tried hard to not show the depth of her knowledge on a daily basis. When questions were asked of her, instead of rattling off the answer, she would go do the research and then return with the answer she already knew. She was doing a good job of hiding her knowledge but was starting to get some recognition for being able to get to the answer quicker than most of the other assistants.

At about the same time as I was getting promoted, she was called into the Dean's office for a discussion. He had been keeping an eye on her based on the input of her guiding professor. He wanted to understand her research methodology and thinking to see what she was doing differently. Could what she did be taught to others?

Of course, she couldn't just tell him that she knew the answer before starting the research so she had to make up a story. She talked about how she came up with a hypothesis, did some high level research in the library and online and then used this to refine her hypothesis or to throw it out. She then continued this methodology until the answer revealed itself. She felt that by looking at the problem from different angles and getting a different perspective, she was able to more rapidly encounter the solutions. In truth, this was how she attacked research when she didn't have the answer.

The Dean listened quietly while she talked. He had a mind like a steel trap so no notes were required. He thanked EL for spending the time with him and sent her on her way.

The following Monday, she was asked back to the Dean's office. Upon entering, she was surprised to find not only the Dean but four of the five Department Chairs. As she told me, her heart started racing about a mile a minute.

The Dean immediately tried to make her comfortable and introduced her to the others in the room. He had been talking with them about his discussion with her and they had questions he wasn't able to answer. Consequently, he called this meeting for them to be able to ask EL directly. He asked her if that was OK to which she could only say yes.

The conversation with the Department Chairs lasted about 90 minutes. Questions ranged from how did she establish her hypothesis, to when did she discredit her hypothesis, what resources did she use, what search engine did she use and how long she stayed on a particular path before giving up. What was she thinking as she went through the process? Was it replicable? How did she create this methodology and why?

By the time the meeting was over, EL was exhausted. The Department Chairs still had questions but the Dean could see EL was running out of gas. He thanked everyone for their time and dismissed EL. She left uncertain of what the outcome had been and if she had revealed too much information. The biggest drain on her mentally during the meeting was to not slip up and share too much.

Finally, about two weeks after meeting with all the Department Chairs, she was back in the Dean's office. This time, the Dean only had the Department Chair of her department with him. And she was shocked at their proposal.

The Dean asked if she would be willing to work with a small subset of researchers to see if they could be taught her methodology. Talk about a minefield and an honor all at the same time. Their proposal was for EL to work with her Department Chair over the rest of the semester to codify what she did intuitively, putting some structure around her thought process so it could be taught. She would then work with three researchers over the spring semester to see if they could learn her methodology. And if so, they would roll it out to more researchers over time.

So we were now both in high visibility situations when all we had wanted to do was fly under the radar.

CHAPTER 62

The three researchers that were paired with EL in the spring were an interesting mix. The first was from Israel, a place where EL had spent significant time. She was going to have to be careful about what she revealed because she couldn't share all she knew without raising some significant questions. Sara was picked because there is a lot of archeological work being done there.

The second person assigned to the team was from Norway. Sven had been with the University for some time and was their most promising researcher. Over time, he would be the most challenging person to work with. Sven had been chosen because of his past record and his desire to understand the Norse legends.

The final person on the team was Olivia. Olivia came from the Outbacks of Australia. She would be EL's most gifted student. She had only been with the University for a little over a year and was chosen because of her work ethic and the Dean's belief that there were some archeological finds of significance to be found in Australia. It was one of the least explored continents from an archeological perspective and he wanted to be a leading force there.

To begin, EL chose two projects that were new to the University, were of medium importance and most significant, she knew the answer. I'm not sure how she knew the answer but because she knew the answer, she could drive the assumptions and research knowing she would be successful.

The first artifact had been found in Egypt. There was discussion on its background and how it had come to be in Egypt. Using her methodology, she asked each of the three researchers to create two hypothesis on what the artifact was, how it came to be found where is was found and how it played into history. The first hypothesis was to have religious overtones and the second hypothesis was to have secular overtones.

The results from the three of them were all unique and the team ended up with six different hypotheses. Not surprisingly, the hypothesis closest to the real answer was from Sara. It was her growing up in close proximity to the find that allowed her to bring her beliefs into creating her solution.

The second artifact came from Germany. In this case, EL asked each of the three to again create two hypotheses with one having a Roman overtone and the second not having any Roman overtone. When they came back together, they found that Sven and Olivia had very similar hypothesis with Roman overtones so they were asked to merge their thoughts and create one unified thought. So with this article, they would have five working hypotheses.

The four of them spent the next month arguing the merits of each solution with the goal to get from the original five or six down to two options. Once they got to two options, they would then dig deeper.

So after two months of work, they had agreed on two hypotheses for each of the artifacts. EL then set up a review with the Department Chair to have her team present an update. Each of the four would have one hypothesis to present. EL's goal in these presentations was to reinforce the methodology to the Chair, reinforce buy in of the methodology in the researchers and garner support for their continued research.

For thirty minutes, the Department Chair sat quietly while they presented. This was significant because he was known for constantly interrupting presenters and not letting them get to their conclusions. EL was becoming very concerned that this was the end of the road for this experiment. After thirty minutes, the Chair stood up and asked them to stop the presentation and to stay in the room until he returned. All four of them bowed their heads dejectedly when he left the room and none had the courage to start a conversation while he was out.

The Chair returned fifteen minutes later with a few surprise guests. He brought back with him his boss the Dean along with two other Department Chairs. Once the four of them were seated, he spoke. "I have asked the three of you to join me for the next hour. What you are going to hear is remarkable. For the past thirty minutes I have sat silently, yes I was silent for the whole time, listening to these four folks led by EL." Turning to EL and her team, he continued "I would like you to start over from the beginning."

Starting over, the team presented for forty five minutes and answered questions for another thirty. The meeting would have continued for much longer but the Dean and the two other Department Chairs were now late for appointments which needed to be addressed.

With the formal meeting over, their Department Chair asked them to join him at the pub to continue his questions and talk about how to move forward. EL came home a little high. I'm not sure if it was from the alcohol or the euphoria of success but it didn't matter.

CHAPTER 63

El and I have talked about when the troubles began to happened in our town but neither of us can pinpoint any one event. It was just something that happened a little bit at a time. Sort of like watching the grass grow. It doesn't seem to be growing and then one morning you wake up and realize it desperately needs to be mowed.

The troubles came in three categories. There were troubles in the streets. There were troubles at the University. And there were troubles at my work.

The troubles in the street were attributed to the worldwide escalation of jihad. But this only covered some of it. South Africa still had lingering feelings from apartheid which had been suppressed because the economy was functioning well. As the global economy began to falter with its ripple effects in South Africa, tensions began to rise. This was the perfect time for restless individuals to band together to cause mayhem. They used multiple cover stories – lingering injustices from apartheid, jihad, normal student demonstrations with their 'rite of passage' to have their voice heard and there were some true grievances which large numbers of people got behind.

The University also presented some challenges. It seemed like every weekend a different group was marching on the campus for some injustice. But when closely observed, it was noticed that about 80% of the marchers were the same and the leaders of each march seemed to rotate amongst three or four instigators. Once this was realized, the local police took action and the troubles seemed to mitigate.

More concerning was EL's work. Over the two years she had been leading and teaching the research teams, her renown had started to grow. For two people who were trying to live under the radar, this wasn't in the plan. It came to a head when one of the most attended conferences for researchers reached out to the University to ask them to be the Keynote speaker. With the request in hand, the University President headed to the Dean's office. They decided EL was the person to represent the University. She was mortified to realize that she was being asked to present to folks who could know her from her past. She tried everything she could but neither the Dean nor the President were budging on their request/demand for her to represent them.

I was having the same success at my work as EL was having at the University. I implemented process improvements at the food processing plant which allowed us to increase production by about 50% without having to hire any additional staff or purchase any equipment. We then invested some of the savings into new equipment which gave us another 30% bump in production. Along the way, I found some mechanical deficiencies in the equipment and worked with the manufacturer to get these corrected.

After the third time that I worked with the manufacturer to make corrections to their equipment, they asked our owner if he and I would talk at their annual conference. My owner was hesitant until the manufacturer reminded him that the conference would be in Paris starting the day after the end of the Tour de France and the manufacturer had seats within 100 yards of the finish line. The deal was done.

Unfortunately, I also knew that it might be possible to run into some of the folks I used to work with so EL and I were facing a hard decision. Our choice of hiding in South Africa was becoming less likely. Our only saving grace was that it had been 5+ years since we had officially died.

CHAPTER 64

My conference came first and we figured it would be more low key than EL's conference. Consequently, we decided to give it a go and see what happened. I also talked the owner into bringing EL along to enjoy the Tour de France.

The time before the conference was very enjoyable. Being able to watch the end of the Tour was a dream come true. EL and I spent some time alone and enjoyed the crowds, the lights and the food. Especially the food.

One thing EL and I had worked hard on during our time in South Africa was to sound like a native when speaking. Over the years, we were able to get to the point of fooling even the locals with the keenest ear. This would pay dividends for both EL and I.

The conference had about 150 attendees from across the globe with about 20 from the United States. I had been able to get an advanced copy of the attendees and saw one name that I recognized. I had worked with Phillip in my early days in Washington DC but hadn't seen him in over 25 years. My hope was that he wouldn't have as good a memory as I did.

My talk went well. I spoke on how the end users can work with the manufacturer to correct problems and also provide suggestions for improvements. I walked through how I had built trust with the design engineers, how we had collaborated in making the changes and how the changes improved our processes. I shared the stage with the manufacturer's lead engineer. He talked about the relationship from his perspective and how our interactions not only improved the areas I addressed but how these changes could affect other pieces of equipment. His team was able to find two additional areas to apply the improvements. In the end, our collaboration was a win for both companies. I might be biased, but I think it was the best presentation of the day.

The day was uneventful until cocktail hour when I was approached by Phillip. He congratulated me on my work and commented on the presentation. After more small talk, he broached the subject of me looking like someone he worked with some years previous. We talked about my "age" and he realized that I would have been 5 years old when he thought I worked with him. His curiosity seemed satisfied though I believe he still had lingering doubts.

The good news is that I got through my conference undetected.

CHAPTER 65

One of the things I loved about EL was her hair. Her deep, deep red hair was unique. I had seen a lot of women with red hair but none came close to EL's color. As we were getting closer to her conference, the discussion started on whether or not she should dye her hair. It just broke my heart to think that she was going to ruin it. After much pouting on my part and some compromise on her part, we settled in on her cutting her hair short and wearing a wig.

Our thought was to arrive at the conference with her new hairstyle and spring it on the Dean and everyone else. But Mary came up with a better suggestion. Why not start talking about it at work, tell her coworkers she wanted to change her hair color, get her hair cut, buy three wigs and have a fun contest. She could continue to wear the wigs at the conference, confusing folks there without confusing the Dean. Mary's plan was a stroke of genius.

We also talked about whether I should accompany her. The conference was going to be in Geneva, one of the cities that EL and I had on our bucket list. But with a large contingency of folks who had known EL coming to the conference, we didn't want to provide too many clues to our past. Consequently, I had to stay home and let EL venture out alone.

On the first day of the conference, EL saw and successfully avoided two folks who she had worked closely with. During dinner that evening, an older couple joined them from Israel. Mary had worked with the husband a few times and the good news was that he didn't recognize her. With blond hair and an Afrikaner accent, Mary was the perfect 30 something.

The true test came the next day during her presentation. The first day, most of the breakout sessions EL had attended had between 25-50 attendees so EL was thinking her session would have about the same number of people. Unfortunately, that wasn't the case. Her session ended up being standing room only with north of 150 attendees.

What she presented was well received. Her question and answer section created a lively debate about her methodology. The questions were so numerous that they had to move the following session to a new room because they couldn't get the crowd at her session out of the room.

During the session, EL had continually scanned the crowd for people paying exceptional attention to her and she found two. One was Rebecca, a wise old lady from Sweden that she had interacted with on multiple occasions. Rebecca had this knack of seeing right through problems and getting to the heart of the matter. She was a quiet person but when she spoke, you knew you needed to listen. The other was Sol, one of the researchers from where she had worked in Washington DC.

As the crowd broke up, EL was relieved to see Rebecca leaving but that was not the case with Sol. He approached her with the comment of "you remind me of someone I used to work with". They talked for some time and finally EL was able to convince Sol that she was just someone who looked a lot like his previous work mate. One disaster averted.

The rest of the day, EL didn't interact with anyone else who thought they recognized her. When she called that evening, she shared her experiences and was grateful that she hadn't come under the close scrutiny of Rebecca. It had been a great day and some very needed recognition had come to the University and the Dean was excited.

The final day of the conference was a gloomy day in Geneva. EL headed down to breakfast knowing that in six hours she would be on a plane home. As she sat down for a quick breakfast, Rebecca appeared out of nowhere and asked if she could join her. Rebecca wanted to talk about EL's methodology and they had a spirited conversation for the entire breakfast. At the end of the conversation and just as Rebecca was excusing herself, she turned and quietly spoke to EL. "Your secret is safe with me. I am one of the Few. There are only three of us left now and we are here to serve you in your time of need. Do not be afraid to ask us for help for HE has told us of you." And with that, she was gone.

CHAPTER 66

I was still in shock when I arrived home. I shared with Tom everything that happened except about Rebecca. I wasn't sure how to tell him about her without first talking with Mary. After Tom fell asleep, I lay awake for a long time thinking and praying. My mind was unsettled and my heart was heavy.

The next morning when Tom left for work, I started sharing with Mary. When I told her about the Few, she was speechless, which if you knew Mary was a once in a lifetime event. "Do you remember anything about the Few?" I asked Mary.

She thought for a long time before responding. "I remember Father giving us a talk many years ago. He said that there would be people in the world who we wouldn't recognize but who knew of us. Their numbers were few and they would become known to us when it was time. He revealed to the Few to become visible. I know there is more but I can't remember. What about you?"

"I remember some of that Mary but I also remember the part about they would only become known in a time of great need. I know that He will watch out for us but their appearance scares me. What is our great need?"

"I'm scared also EL. I think we need to be more vigilant now about our surroundings and also plan for change. We might be ok here but we may need to move somewhere else. I also think you need to reach back out to Rebecca."

"You are right Mary. We need to put into place a plan and I need to reach back to Rebecca. But how do I tell Tom?"

"Just tell Tom that Rebecca is someone you made friends with who wants more advice on what you are doing. If you make your connection to Rebecca all about work, there won't be any suspicion on his part."

"I can't remember if I talked about Rebecca from Sweden though in my earlier work. What if I did and Tom remembers?"

"Just call her Becca and don't mention where she is from. The names are different enough that hopefully he won't make the connection."

"Ok" I said with a heavy heart. We were keeping a lot of information from Tom and one more thing was not something I was looking forward to.

With false bravado, I told Mary that I would give Rebecca a call today, that we needed to spend some serious time in prayer and we would reconvene tomorrow after Tom left for work. She agreed and I headed off towards the University.

CHAPTER 67

Rebecca and I played phone tag throughout the day and never connected. It was frustrating because my anxiety level continued to rise with each failed interaction. By the time I got home, I was pretty wired up.

Tom could see my state of disarray and did his best to help but it only made it worse because I couldn't talk with him. I needed some alone time with Mary. Tom's incessant tries to help, along with that smile that won my heart many years ago, started to break through my mood. A few glasses of wine also helped.

Tom was making dinner when I realized that Mary was nowhere to be found. I asked Tom if he had seen her and he said "Oh. She left a note on the table about heading out to visit Yosef for a few days. Here you go," as he handed me the note.

I was furious. At Tom for forgetting to tell me. At Mary for going on one of her sex romps. What was she thinking? I could just strangle them both. More wine and Tom's smile didn't help. After a quite dinner, Tom suggested I head in for bath. Maybe a hot bath and bubbles would help. It didn't, well maybe just a little but I'm not going to admit it.

CHAPTER 68

The next morning, Mary called on my way to work. I went off on her. How could she be thinking of her libido at a time like this? What was she thinking? She should be helping solve this mystery.

Mary listened patiently while I dumped all my frustrations on her. She even asked if I was done, to which I said NO and started off again.

After about five minutes, I had finally run out of anger for the time being. Once I was done, Mary calmly asked "Do you know where I'm headed?" and off I went for a third time.

At this point, Mary lost her cool and screamed at me to just stop. Mary never screams. Mary never raises her voice at least not to me. And this shocked me into silence.

Mary then asked again "Do you know where I am headed? Do you know why I am headed to see Yosef"?

Based on the silence, Mary assumed the answer to both of these questions was no. So she enlightened me.

Yosef was her friend in **Jerusalem**, which she emphasized. He had been a **longtime** friend, to which she emphasized longtime. He had helped her with **research** in the past, to which she emphasized research. And then all of a sudden it became perfectly clear.

I said "Mary you are brilliant. Why didn't I think of that?"

To which Mary replied "You think with your heart EL. I think with my head. I know you don't give me a lot of credit for my thinking but I do come up with a good idea every now and then."

I apologized to Mary for doubting her and we had a good cry together even though we were miles apart. Fortunately, I had made it to the University parking lot by now so I didn't have to worry about hitting anyone or anything with the car. I don't cry and drive very well.

Mary said she would be back in 3-4 days and encouraged me to continue my research. I promised I would re-double my efforts and we could compare notes when she got back home.

CHAPTER 69

It was another full day before Rebecca and I were able to sync up. I was just starting my lunch hour when she rang me up. I didn't have any plans for the hour so we were able to have a long conversations.

I had so many questions for her and I didn't know where to start. I had been thinking about this now for almost a week and settled on my first question – "Why now?"

Before Rebecca answered she needed to ask me a few questions. "How is Tom's health? Why are we in South Africa? Have I been listening?"

My answers were "Tom's health continues to be perfect. He hasn't been sick a day since we got married. His work is going well, we run, we exercise together, we do everything we should do to stay healthy."

"We are in South Africa because we needed to start over in a place where no one would know us. We wanted to live in a country that spoke English and where we could blend in from a language and physical characteristic perspective. South Africa fit all our criteria."

"Have I been listening to whom?" was my response to the third question. "I listen to a lot of folks."

After a long pause Rebecca started. "I am sorry to hear about Tom's health. That is a complication that we will have to deal with." I was offended and was ready to go off on Rebecca when she continued. "You are probably offended by that statement but it will become obvious to you why I say that."

She continued with "South Africa is ok but not ideal. This will continue to be a discussion point between us and you will have to make a decision."

Finally she said "Have you been listening to Him? He has been reaching out to you and Mary but you aren't listening. You two need to spend more time in prayer." And then it became clear of whom she was speaking.

"Where is Mary?" she asked.

"Mary is spending 3-4 days with a friend. I expect her home by the weekend. Why?"

"When Mary is home and you have Heard, we will have our next call. Make sure Mary is with you for our next call. I will know when it is time, because He will tell me, and I will call you."

And with that, she hung up.

I sat there in silence for a long time. And then I wept.

CHAPTER 70

Mary's trip ended up being five anxious days. While she was gone, we didn't talk because the subject was private and we didn't want anyone listening in. In today's world, I was choosing to be skeptical.

While Mary was gone, I spent a lot of time in prayer. Unfortunately, I wasn't getting many answers which was frustrating. But I have learned over the years that He will be there when the time is right. What I did discover though was that my prayer life had gone a little soft. Never a good thing.

Mary got home late Friday afternoon just about the time Tom came home from work. Tom had had a stellar week at work and wanted to celebrate. Yeah! All I wanted to do was go off in a corner and talk with Mary and Tom wants to have fun. In hindsight, the time of celebration was a good thing. It forced me to reevaluate my situation and also the wine helped me wind down. It also gave me a good excuse on why I needed to get back up after joining Tom in bed.

With Tom gently snoring, more like purring, I headed out to talk with Mary. I thought she would be all fired up and ready to talk, only to find her asleep also. Never the most patient person, I woke Mary up to talk.

Yosef. Ah Yosef. He was as good as always. Mary started to go into the details until she saw the look on my face. She rolled her eyes and said that I never wanted to listen to the good parts.

The primary reason for visiting Yosef was that he was in Jerusalem. In Jerusalem were archives and safe houses that had been employed over many centuries that needed exploring and Yosef was a good cover besides being good for the libido.

What Mary found was both exciting and discouraging. Everything she read said that the time of Revelation was getting closer. There were more events happening in the world that lined up with the Scriptures though some key events were still missing. No clear direction was coming until the day before Mary was scheduled to come home.

While doing research in one of the safe houses, she was visited by an old rabbi. She hadn't noticed him right away but came to realize that he had been patiently watching her for a few hours. He would sit in a chair that was visible to her and pray, looking her way every now and then to ensure that she was still there. Once she had to move to a different room to access additional books and he came into the room and resumed his prayers.

As Mary was getting up to leave, the rabbi approached and asked if they could talk. With all the events that were happening, Mary was aware enough that she needed to take the time. The rabbi told her to follow and he started off. They walked through Jerusalem for about 20 minutes in silence with Mary getting both anxious and pissed at the same time. About the time she was ready to explode, the rabbi opened a small, unseen door into what had to be the smallest, oldest synagogue she had ever seen. The rabbi asked her to sit and pray before disappearing.

Mary prayed and it was magical. Never before had she beheld the chorus of angels she saw. They sang with such beauty, beauty beyond our words. And she found herself crying with joy. The singing stopped and death and destruction prevailed. And again she cried but with tears of sadness. When the visions stopped, a clear voice could be hear. "It is time. You must decide." And then silence and calm.

Shortly afterward, the old rabbi returned. He said it was time for Mary to go and that it was an honor to have met her and be able to serve. His family had waited many lifetimes for today. Upon leaving, Mary realized that she had been in the synagogue for almost three hours.

Wow was all I could say, as I sat in stunned silence.

CHAPTER 71

Mary asked what I had found out from Rebecca. I told her how the discussion had not really been a discussion but more of a one sided, motherly advice session from Rebecca.

Mary and I agreed that our prayer life had fallen off over the past few years. We had become complacent in our world and forgotten our real purpose. Life with Tom, with the three of us together, was the family setting we had never really experienced. Even though we didn't have children, we functioned as a family. And it has been magical.

We talked about what the two visions meant. We had each seen the chorus of angels before though Mary guaranteed we had never seen anything like what she saw. In our hearts, we knew that this meant peace, love, joy, happiness and grace.

Neither of us had ever seen anything like what Mary described around the death and destruction. Was this the fire and brimstone from Revelations?

Mary then remembered to share what she learned on The Few. She had spent almost three full days reading through our private archives along with the archives of trusted associates. In the end she was frustrated because what she found was very little. All she could find was one reference which said that The Few would make themselves known when the mother was in need of them most.

And then we talked about my discussion with Rebecca. What did she mean when she said that Tom's health was a complication we would have to deal with? I think we both knew but neither one of us was willing to voice our opinions.

Why was South Africa only ok? Did it have cooties we weren't aware of? We both realized it was a little isolated but that was some of its beauty.

We finished comparing our notes with more questions than answers. We decided to both spend time in prayer over the weekend and continue our discussion on Monday after Tom left for work.

I headed to bed but sleep didn't come. Too many unanswered questions kept running through my brain for me to unwind. After a few hours, I finally decided to "let go and let God" take over. Eight am came pretty early when Tom, all refreshed, woke me up for our morning run. Ugh.

CHAPTER 72

It was a beautiful weekend. The weather was absolutely perfect. Back in the United States, we used to call this a Chamber of Commerce day. The temperature was 75 degrees Fahrenheit, the wind was blowing at about 10 miles per hour, the sky was cloudless and there was this smell of flowers in the air. On Sunday afternoon, I mentioned to Mary that this weekend reminded me of the farm when we were growing up.

Though the weather was special and Tom was his normal everyday great guy, I wasn't really enjoying myself. For some reason, this was the weekend that Tom wanted to do everything together. So with only 80% of my mind and body committed, I did the best I could do.

I put on a good face and I don't think Tom realized that my mind was never fully engaged. I continued to think about the events of the last few weeks and couldn't shake the feeling that Mary and I were missing something.

And the bad part of it was that Mary and I couldn't talk.

Monday finally came and Tom headed off to work with a big grin on his face. I could tell he had had a lot of fun over the weekend and was totally reenergized. My classes were on Monday, Wednesday and Friday so I was out the door right behind Tom after telling Mary that it was her job to pray for the both of us today.

My head wasn't into school on Monday. I had a hard time focusing on the lessons I had prepared for the students. So instead of trying to force bad teaching, I decided to use a technique one of my professors had used in one of my classes. I asked each of the students to list one piece of knowledge they learned during the class that they would tell a prospective student. What was the most important thing they had learned. I gave the students 5 minutes to write down their advice and turn the paper into me. I then read each answer anonymously and we talked about it. It was enlightening to both me and the class the number of different answers we received. All in all, it was a worthwhile technique I decided I would use again. Thanks Professor Smith.

Tuesday after Tom left for work, Mary and I finally had some time alone to talk. We shared with each other only to realize that none of us had experienced an epiphany since the last time we talked. Not really knowing what to do next, we held each other's hands and prayed.

As we sat silently holding hands praying, I was filled with the Holy Spirit. Never before had I beheld the chorus of angels I saw. They sang with such beauty, beauty beyond our words. And I found myself crying with joy. The singing stopped and death and destruction prevailed. And again I cried but with tears of sadness. When the visions stopped, a clear voice could be hear. "It is time. You must decide." And then silence and calm.

I opened my eyes to see Mary holding me, cradling me and rocking me. I had been in a semi-trance for almost three hours. I told her what I saw and we both started crying. I had seen what she had seen. We still didn't know what it meant but we now knew it was important.

For most of the rest of the day, we just sat together wanting to touch each other for reassurance.

Mary and I struggled through the week. No more visions, no answered prayers and nothing from Rebecca. The only thing remarkable about the week was Tom's comment Friday over dinner. Tom said it was one of the top two or three weeks he had ever experienced both personally and professionally. What a contrast.

CHAPTER 73

Saturday, Mary decided she wanted to join Tom and I on our morning run. She also wanted to go running up in one of the secluded mountain areas that was about an hour outside of town. Since Tom and I were both surprised and pleased that Mary wanted to join us, we were more than willing to go where she wanted to go.

We packed a cooler with sandwiches, protein bars, fruit and plenty of liquid and headed out. We figured that after our run, we would find a nice place to have a picnic lunch.

Our normal Saturday run was between five and eight miles but Tom was starting to build up mileage for the marathon he planned to run in three weeks. Neither Mary nor I wanted to do the thirteen miles Tom was hoping for so we talked about how to get Tom extra mileage.

When we got to the trailhead, we found that one of the trails was 1.5 miles up to a lake, 5 miles around the lake and 1.8 miles back using a different trail. If we all ran around the lake once and Tom ran around the lake twice, we could all meet our objectives.

The run around the lake continued to add to Tom's "top two or three weeks ever" and I had to agree that the run was spectacular. When we got back to the trailhead, Mary and I found a place to rest while Tom started around again. We had timed ourselves the first time around and it had taken us about 40 minutes to get around. We both set timers on our watch and if Tom wasn't back in 40 minutes, Mary and I would start running the loop backwards to give him encouragement. Tom had his phone but the coverage was spotty to non-existent.

Mary and I found an overlook where you could see the whole lake. The sun sparkled off the water as the wind formed ripples. The trees swayed gently and I was again reminded of the farm when we were growing up. I held Mary's hand to get her attention and tell her about the farm and it was as if that connection between us set it off.

The lake was covered in a chorus of angels singing the song that was so, so beautiful. And then the angels were replaced with a sea of red from the dead and dying. And then Gabriele appeared saying it is time. Mary and I must decide. And he was gone.

His departure brought both of us out of our trance and instantly I knew what this vision and the previous vision meant. I looked into Mary's eyes and saw that she knew also. And then at the same time we both screamed Tom!

CHAPTER 74

It has been about 55 minutes since Tom left for his second loop, so he was late. We both had this sense of doom and I could see the fear in Mary's eyes. We decided to break up and each run the path in opposite directions and then that seemed stupid. If Tom was just a few hundred yards down the path one way or the other, one of us would be running five miles. Also, if there was something on the trail that attacked Tom, we would be just as vulnerable. And finally, when we did find him, both of us would be needed to get him out.

So we each ran the loop in our minds trying to pinpoint where we thought Tom could have trouble. At almost the same time, we both yelled out the steep downhill stretch about four miles into the loop. We decided to run the loop backwards hoping this would get us to Tom the fastest.

We sprinted up the path. In less than a five minutes, we both realized we couldn't maintain the pace and we both needed a short walk. Once we caught our breadth, we continued to run as fast as we could knowing we needed to maintain the pace for some time.

When we got to the steep part of the trail, there was no Tom. Both of our hearts sank and you could hear them crash against the trail.

We were just about to start running when Mary thought she heard something. We both tried to stand quietly, which is hard to do when you are panting for breath. And then I heard it also. It was coming from off into the woods towards the lake. Mary and I both pointed that we needed to go that way but neither of us were too sure about the circumstances.

Using standard military tactics, we spread far enough apart that it would be hard for someone to surprise both of at the same time. Creeping along, we headed towards the lake.

About ten yards in, Mary found Tom and screamed to me. Tom had a compound fracture on his right leg and there was some serious bleeding. Somehow, he had gotten his shirt off and used it as a tourniquet to stop the bleeding before passing out.

Tom was in need of medical assistance. We both looked at our cell phones and there was no coverage on either phone. Mary volunteered to run back to the fork in the trail where there was some coverage and back to the car if needed, while I stayed with

Tom. Before leaving, Mary helped me drag Tom out to the trail. She took off like a woman possessed.

All I could do was sit on the ground and hold Tom. Between tears and prayer, I would run my fingers through his hair and tell him I loved him so much.

It took Mary a little over an hour to arrive with help. First on the scene was a paramedic panting and sweating from a long run. It looked like Mary had pushed him hard up the trail. He came prepared with a bag of blood and got that flowing into Tom's system. He then began to assess the damage to the leg.

Ten minutes after the first paramedic arrived, three more showed up with a stretcher. You could tell by the sweat poring off their bodies that they had been pushing hard up the trail also. They loaded Tom onto the stretcher and we started the long walk back to the ambulance. It took us almost forty five minutes to walk the 2.5 miles to the trail head. Tom remained semi-comatose just as he had since we first found him.

I jumped into the ambulance with Tom and Mary drove the car. We drove at a breakneck speed to the hospital where Tom was rushed into surgery.

Ninety minutes later the surgeon came out to tell us that Tom was stable, the broken leg had been reset and the leg put in a cast but that Tom would need to stay in the hospital at least overnight.

Mary and I were exhausted. We both still had our running cloths on and were stinky and downright unpresentable. The surgeon assured us that Tom would be unconscious for the next few hours and encouraged us to go home and freshen up. We thanked the surgeon for all he had done and headed out to make the thirty minute drive home.

As we were leaving the surgeon said "by the way, you two were remarkable today. He should have died out on the trail and he lived today only because of your intervention." We should have been happy by his statement but instead we were both crushed knowing the unintended consequences.

Halfway home, my cell phone rang. It was Rebecca. In a motherly stern voice, she asked "what happened today? Are you and Mary both OK? Why is your blood in the system? You know this cannot happen.

CHAPTER 75

I was stunned. Why was Rebecca calling? What was she talking about? What did she mean by our blood is in the system? Of course I knew Mary and I couldn't ever go to a hospital. Our blood would mark us as very, very unique.

I handed the phone to Mary and she put it on speaker. We told Rebecca that Mary and I were OK and that neither one of had blood drawn. And then a light bulb went off – Tom?

We shared with Rebecca our adventures today and how Tom needed to have surgery. That he was going to be fine with proper recovery. And that we were on our way home from the hospital to get cleaned up.

She wanted to know if either of us had bled. A big NO.

She wanted to know if either of us had donated blood. Another big NO.

She was silent for a long time and then said she would call us back. She needed to do some research but for us to keep the phone handy. Oh, and to burn any clothes with blood on them after soaking them in bleach. And then she hung up.

Mary and I looked at each other like, "What just happened". What access did Rebecca have? How did she even know something happened?

We stopped on the way home to get the bleach. Mary had to go into the store because I still had blood on my clothes and we didn't want to attract any more attention.

Upon getting home, we stripped down and threw all the clothes into the sink to soak in bleach. We figured it was better to be safe than sorry and didn't want a stray drop of blood to be left hanging around. Mary headed to her shower and me to mine to get cleaned up.

I was toweling off when the phone rang. It was Rebecca. She said to get Mary on the phone also so the two of us were standing around listening to Rebecca with just towels on.

Rebecca started off slow. She asked if we both knew that there were particles in our blood which were unique to any other human. We both agreed that we knew.

She asked if we both knew that if researchers were to get their hands on this blood that major changes would happen to the human race. Again we both agreed that we knew.

She then said that a small subset of those unique particles were identified in Tom's blood. Both Mary and I had to pick our jaws up off the floor, our mouths were open that far. All we could do was mumble something like "OH?".

And then it came back to me on how I had healed Tom that first night. I must have changed something in his genetic make-up. But I couldn't say anything to Rebecca. It was too long of a story.

Rebecca started talking. She had someone cleaning up the database. Tom's information would be "lost", wiped from the database as if they never appeared. More troublesome were the actual samples at the hospital. The good news was that it was a small hospital and should be fairly easy to breach that evening. Tom's samples, along with a host of others, would be taken. But once the samples were discovered missing, the hospital would begin again to collect them.

She said Tom needed to be removed from the hospital as soon as possible. And no later than tomorrow at 7:00 am. That is when the missing blood would most likely be discovered.

We were instructed to bring Tom home. We were also instructed to be prepared to travel.

She asked if we clearly understood our instructions and the ramifications if they weren't followed. She didn't relent until we both said yes.

Mary and I looked at each other in stunned silence for a long time. Mary then said that we had better get dressed and head back to the hospital. We could talk along the way.

CHAPTER 76

No sooner had we got on the highway headed to the hospital and the phone rang. It was Rebecca. Mary answered the phone and put it on speaker.

"EL. You and Tom will be leaving on a 2:30 pm flight tomorrow for Chicago. Tom's mother was in a serious car accident and she is not expected to live. They are asking Tom to come home as quickly as possible."

I said "what are you talking about? Tom's mother died years ago. And besides, Tom is not going to be ready to fly by tomorrow."

"Well I needed a cover story on why the two of you are leaving the country so quickly. I also needed a destination that you could travel to without having to waste time on getting a visa. This seemed the most convenient story and the easiest to create a cover for so you will just need to run with it."

"Regarding Tom, you do not have a choice. You either leave tomorrow or Tom ends up in an institution for the rest of his life, studied as if he were some kind of freak. Are we clear?"

She didn't wait for an answer. "Pack as much as you can in two suitcases each. Make sure to take all, and I mean all your valuables including what is in the safe deposit box. You need to leave most of your items behind just like you would if you were only going on a two week vacation."

"Why do we need to take all our valuables? And the bank isn't open on Sunday so I won't be able to get into our safe deposit box." I said.

"You need to take all your valuables because you are not coming back. Tom's accident does not allow you to be on the grid any longer in South Africa."

She then continued as if the subject was closed and no more questions were allowed. "You and Tom have a layover and plane change in Sydney, Australia. This will force you to collect your bags and transport them between airlines."

"If they are going to the United States, can't you just get them a straight through flight?" Mary asked.

"I could do that if they were really going to the United States. I need the US location to get them out of South Africa. Now let me continue."

"Because of Tom's condition, you will need assistance to get between airlines. Padra will meet you with a wheelchair once you get off the airline. She will assist in getting your bags. Once these have been claimed, she will provide you both with new identities and you will use these to enter Australia. Once you have cleared customs, Padra will take you to a safe location."

"Where are we going?" I asked.

"For now, this is all you need to know."

"Finally EL, you will need to call the University and Tom's work to let them know about Tom's mother. Do not share anything about Tom's running accident with either party. Tell them you are leaving on Monday and probably returning in about two weeks."

"Do you understand these instructions EL?"

I said "yes, but you just said we were leaving tomorrow, Sunday?"

"Think smokescreen EL. I need your head in the game here. And who is meeting you in Sydney? This is critical."

I had to run back through the conversation to come up with the name. I said Padra.

"She will introduce herself to you. If anyone else offers help, graciously decline. Understood!"

Again I said yes but in the back of my mind all I could think about was how did this all happen.

She then turned her attention to Mary.

"Mary, you have been living under the radar. Very few people know who you are but your neighbors will be able to guess that you are EL's sister and some may confuse you for her. Consequently, you must leave also."

"I had you leaving tomorrow also but you will need to stay until Monday now to clear out the safe deposit box."

We heard her give some instructions to someone else before she continued.

"You are to take EL and Tom to the airport. Once you drop them off, you are to drive directly to the Marriott Hotel at the airport. Valet park the car and act as if you are checking in. Do not let the bellhops take your bags. Upon entering the hotel, you will be met by Patrick. You will challenge him regarding his name and he will correctly apologize and say his proper name is Timothy

Patrick. Only after he provides you with this information can you trust him."

"You and he will be traveling as Mr. and Mrs. O'Reily. He will help you with the safe deposit box if it is safe for you to enter the bank. Otherwise, we will find another way to get its contents. Are you clear on your instructions Mary?"

The look on Mary's face was priceless and all she could do was mumble out a yes. Which wasn't sufficient for Rebecca. She pressed Mary until Mary clearly said yes along with repeating the instructions on how to meet Timothy Patrick.

Rebecca was ready to hang up but I got one question in. "Why all this?"

Rebecca took a long, cleansing breath before answering. "There have been dark forces pursuing you for many, many years that want to stop you. Until now, you two have been able to stay ahead of them. But Tom's blood has mobilized them and now speed is of the essence."

"Have you two seen visions?" to which we both said yes.

"Those visions represent what is at stake over the next few days. Are we clear on the importance of our actions?"

In subdued voices both Mary and I said yes.

Rebecca continued "one final thing. Dr. Jones will meet you at the hospital. Follow only his directions. You should be checked out of the hospital in less than 30 minutes after arriving. If it takes longer than that or Dr. Jones is not available, take Tom, leave the hospital, do not go home and call me immediately."

"Good luck and God bless" is all she said before hanging up just as we drove into the hospital parking lot.

CHAPTER 77

As I was walking into the hospital, the phone rang. It was Rebecca.

"Don't go to the bank."

"Why? We saw a branch not far from the hospital. Mary decided to run to the bank while I worked with Dr. Jones."

"Shit" was all I heard as the phone went silent.

30 seconds later, Mary's phone rang. It was Rebecca.

"Don't use EL or Tom's identification at the bank. They have a tap on their account and would be there in minutes."

"OK thanks. I'll head back to the hospital without accessing their accounts" Mary replied.

"By the way, who is 'they' that you keep talking about?" asked Mary.

"Who they are is not important. What is important is that you all don't run across them. Now get your money, pick up EL and Tom and head to the address I am going to text to you. Do not go back to your apartment. And throw away EL and Tom's phones. No, give those phones to Dr. Jones. Keep your phone." With those words of encouragement, the phone went dead.

Mary told me that she was able to withdraw $8,750 dollars. The teller was talkative and wanted to know what she was going to do with the money. She thought of being snippy with the teller but didn't want to draw attention to herself. She said that her boyfriend and her were putting up a new fence to keep in their dog. It had recently jumped the short fence they had and run off twice and they were tired of chasing it down. The story went over well enough that the teller shared a story of her dog running away also.

Mary also updated me on the conversation with Rebecca. I started asking a bunch of questions to which Mary just held up her hands. She didn't have any more answers than I did so it wasn't fair to pick on her.

Tom looked like crap. He was still groggy from surgery. He was in pain and he couldn't really walk.

Dr. Jones had all the paperwork ready for us when I arrived. As everyone knows that has ever tried to help someone check out of the hospital, even with the paperwork done, it still takes 30 minutes to get from the room to the car. I think part of nurse training is teaching them how to slow down the discharge process.

Dr. Jones' advice to us was that Tom would be in severe pain for the next 48 hours. He should stay on the pain pills for at least that long but could stay on them for up to five days. His broken bones had be set and would need six week to heal so the cast should stay on for at least that long. He was against us taking him out of the hospital but it was our choice.

As we were leaving, I started to dig for my cell phone to give to Dr. Jones. I glanced at Mary and saw her give me that slight headshake no, so I pretended I was digging for my keys only to remember that Mary had them.

When we got Tom loaded into the car I asked Mary where we were headed to. She showed me her phone which had a note that said "Follow my lead" and then answered "I need to pick up a few private items from the drug store. My cycle should be starting tomorrow and I don't have any pads. I saw a drug store not far from here that we can stop at."

I headed to the drug store and Mary jumped out. She went inside to buy the items she needed while Tom and I waited in the car. Unknown to me, Mary also called an Uber ride and one of her friends. She came out of the drug store just as the Uber driver and her friend arrived.

She asked her friend if she could drive our car to the University and leave it there. The friend started to question her until Mary just said "please. I'll explain later". She told Tom and me to join her in the Uber car. But before everyone left the parking lot, she made the three of us leave our phones in our car. I was so confused. No car and no phones. What was she thinking? She sent her friend out one end of the parking lot while she directed the Uber car out the other end.

Once in the car, she gave the driver the address to the Nordstrom's store about 15 miles away. He gave us a suspicious look to which Mary smiled and said "we are on an adult scavenger hunt. The three of us always win so no one wanted to play with us anymore. I said we could win with him in a cast and half drunk, no car and no phones. With these conditions, everyone said they would play one more time. We were told to come to this location to start and that we would get our first clue here and that we would end up at the University. That is where our car and phones are headed. Kind of fun huh?"

The Uber driver was comforted. He started engaging Mary in conversation and she flirted with him to no end. No more fears from him.

I figured Mary had picked Nordstrom's because in the same mall was a medical device store. Mary went and rented a wheelchair for Tom so that we had a little more mobility. Once we had Tom in the wheelchair and were inside the mall Mary started talking.

Mary's uncomfortableness started with the timing of Rebecca's calls. How did she get so lucky with making her calls at just the right time? So Mary started watching. Eventually, she noticed the elaborate series of tails that were following us and guessed that Rebecca was not who she said she was or the Rebecca on the phone was not the same person that I met at the conference.

She knew for sure when Dr. Jones had done the discharge incorrectly and the nurse went along with it. She also recognized that the pain pills the doctor had supplied were not the standard pain pills. Final confirmation came when she called the airlines to check on our reservations for tomorrow only to find that no reservations existed. She guessed that they were being led into a trap. Consequently, she took us to the mall where we could talk openly without fear of being overheard or being followed.

It was time to drop off the grid. It had been a long time since we had been in danger and I realized that my reflexes had slowed. I had to get my edge back if we wanted to survive.

Game on.

CHAPTER 78

About 100 yards into the mall, Mary pulled us aside and started digging in her purse. She finally found this little device at the bottom of the purse she was looking for. She then took us into one of the shops to buy a prepaid cell phone. Connecting the little device to the phone created a pretty powerful antenna and she went through the process of dialing what seemed like 20 numbers. After she was done, she said that we were good to go for 5 minutes and we needed to hurry.

I started to question her but she gave me that "we don't have time now to discuss this so please just follow along" look which I had seen before.

We practically ran through the mall to get to the food court. Once there, she punched in a code to get us into the workers area. We walked the back halls until we came to a small door. She again entered the number to open a cypher lock and hurried us in. Looking at her watch, she said we made it with about 15 second to spare.

What I saw was a small room about 10x10 in size with no windows and no other doors other than the one we came in. I'm thinking to myself, "how is this helping", when Mary started talking.

She confessed that while living in South Africa with us, she became concerned that we would need an escape plan. It had not been unusual over the years for us to live a life only to have to end it with no notice and us running for our lives. So she started working on an escape plan.

She reviewed the layout of the city, where major construction sites had been completed and all the hidden connections between buildings. What she found was that this mall was about 100 yards from a series of old catacombs. Those catacombs ran for miles in each direction with the west branch coming up within yards of the train station. We were going to use the catacombs to escape.

I must have given her the dumbest look ever at about the same time Tom asked "so how do we get out of this room?"

Mary ignored my look and Tom's question. She had befriended the owner of the mall, an older lady who was a recluse but was worth many millions of dollars. The owner suspected foul play with how the mall was run and asked Mary to became her "secret shopper" always going through the mall and making reports back. She was given access to every door and every room in the mall.

Mary found this room and claimed it for herself. She installed the cypher lock and was the only one who knew the combination. Once the room was secure, she started making the connection from the mall to the catacombs. Every day, she would come in here to dig and remove the dirt. It had taken her close to a year but she finally broke through.

Tom and I still looked confused and this time I asked "so how do we get out of this room again?"

Mary continued to ignore us. She opened a few of the boxes that were filled with clothes for her and me. She then opened two more boxes with clothes for Tom. She recommended that we all needed a change of clothes and started laying out suggestions for all of us.

She then opened up one more box that contained wigs for the three for us and some facial hair for Tom. She mumbled to herself that the broken leg was something that was going to be hard to hide.

Finally, I stopped her long enough to ask a third time, "how do we get out of this room?"

"Oh. We pull this lever, which was well hidden, which drops these hidden wheels and this section of shelving rolls out. Once inside the tunnel, we pull the shelving back closed and use a matching handle on the inside to raise the hidden wheels."

Tom and I stared at the tunnel she had dug. It was wide enough for us to crawl through but not really wide enough to get the wheelchair though. Tom was in pain and his shoulders visibly sank when he realized that he was not going to have use of it on the other side.

Tom and I decided to dress like street people. We were hoping that this would allow us to better hide his crutches. Mary changed her hair to red and took on the look of a successful business woman.

While changing, Tom asked if Mary had any tools in the room. She opened a well-stocked toolbox and Tom started digging. In about 5 minutes, he had the wheels off the chair and said it should now fit through the tunnel. Why hadn't either of us thought of that?

We picked up the room and put our old clothes in a bag. We would take these, along with the rest of the clothes, with us and leave them in the tunnel. We also put the spare food and water into the tunnel for later use. Mary and I each made a trip with pieces of the wheelchair and then came back for Tom. Once we were all out of the room and it looked pristine again, Mary closed the door.

CHAPTER 79

Once in the catacombs, we stopped to rest and realized how tired we all were. It had been over twelve hours since we had started the morning with a long run and all the ensuing events had drained us to the core. We decided to make camp just outside the tunnel.

Mary dug through the food and made us peanut butter and crackers. She also opened a can of tuna for each of us. It wasn't the most elegant meal but it sure hit the spot.

Mary noticed Tom starting to fall asleep while he was eating so she pulled out the lone sleeping bag for him. We got him situated in the bag and he was asleep before his head hit the floor.

We finished our dinner in silence.

The catacombs were surrealistic. It was so quiet you could hear a pin drop. There was also this low glow that came from somewhere that allowed you to just see each other and also to see down the hallways. The glow was bright enough that you didn't need a flashlight but dim enough that you wanted to reach up and turn up the lights. We didn't see any evidence of mice, snakes or spiders and I was perfectly fine with no critters.

When we were done, Mary gathered up all the food containers. She closed up the crackers and put the left over ones in a sealable plastic bag. She stored them along with the peanut butter back in the food case. The used tuna cans she put in a separate plastic bag to be disposed of or left behind.

We then looked at each other and realized we needed a plan.

I suggested that Mary take off and get out of town before the folks chasing us could find us. Tom and I would find a place to lay low until his leg had healed well enough to travel.

Mary ripped this suggestion to pieces. First, she wasn't going to leave me behind because I was the one they wanted to stop. They needed to stop the upcoming child. Second, my plan would require me to leave Tom unprotected as I moved about to get supplies. And finally, she didn't think there was any place that we could hide for that long without being spotted. Whoever was chasing us was well funded and well connected.

Mary had a much more sophisticated plan which she began to reveal in pieces to me. She recommended that we stay in the catacombs until Tom was no longer in a cast. She felt that we would only need to be here for two to three weeks. When asked why, she said that over the years, she had noticed that Tom healed from accidents two to three times faster than the average human. Based on the evidence from today, she now surmised that when I had originally "healed" Tom on our wedding night, I had also altered his basic healing capabilities. Consequently, she felt that his leg would be healed in less than six weeks.

This she felt gave us a distinct advantage. The bad guys would be expecting us to need to hide for six weeks. If we could manage to survive for the first two to three weeks, we would have three to four weeks of time to be traveling with non-broken leg Tom.

I had to agree with her logic and only hoped it played out in reality.

Over the years and through her many travels, she had also cultivated a series of friends across the world. She had specifically targeted three females who looked enough like herself that when they went out together, people would ask if they were sisters. She had told each of these ladies that she was an international spy and had asked if they would do one or two things for her if she ever needed it. Each of the ladies had thought she was crazy but agreed to help if they were asked. It was Mary's plan to have each of these ladies make a banking transaction to divert attention away from them. The first transaction would happen on Tuesday in Antwerp. This should draw eyes away from South Africa.

Wow! I commented that she had been doing some serious planning. She was gracious in her reply but I knew that I had let us down by just playing husband and wife with Tom over all these years.

My brain was swimming with too much information and I couldn't process any more. We decided to get some sleep while we could. Mary asked me to help her get everything out of the tunnel. Once it was all out, she did something and the tunnel collapsed in on itself. I couldn't believe it, she had just taken away one of our escape routes.

Mary explained that it was not an escape route but a "get captured" route. The bad guys were good at what they did. If they broke into the room and started to do some analysis of the room with x-rays, they would soon find the tunnel and swarm the catacombs. By collapsing the tunnel, x-rays would not reveal anything.

Brilliant was the only word that came to mind.

With that done, Mary pulled out the lone blanket and we snuggled together for warmth.

CHAPTER 80

We both woke with a start. Noises were coming from somewhere and then we realized that Tom had moved down the hallway to take care of the demands Mother Nature inflicted on all of us. This made Mary and I realize we had the same demands.

Tom said he felt a little better though it was hard to tell in the soft light. We had him sit in the wheelchair as Mary dug into her bag of goodies for breakfast. She pulled out three bags of trail mix and three protein bars along with some water for us all to drink. She shared that we would need to find a place to get water as she only had enough for us for today and tomorrow.

During breakfast, Tom started asking questions. They were hard questions which forced Mary and me to tiptoe through the answers.

His first question was "why are people chasing us?"

Mary answered this one. She explained that when he went to the hospital, the analysis of his blood had alerted the international version of the American Center for Disease Control or CDC. The doctor had explained there was a genetic marker in his blood which was similar to a highly contagious disease. They wanted to study Tom and move him to a contamination hospital. We knew that he would never leave the hospital. And with his long lifespan, he would be a prisoner for many, long years.

I was impressed with the story that Mary made up and Tom bought it. He was quiet for a long time while he continued to eat.

His next question was "do we have a plan?" Coming from a military background, he knew we needed a plan.

I took this question on. I explained that we were going to hang out in the catacombs for as long as possible. We hoped that we would be able to stay underground long enough for his leg to heal and him not to need the cast or crutches. Both of them kept him from blending in.

Again he was quiet while continuing to eat.

His next question surprised us. He asked "what are our assets?"

I turned to Mary to answer this one since she knew what she packed. She started listing them off. Food for seven days. Water for 2 days. One sleeping bag. One blanket. One wheelchair. Three changes of clothes for each of us those being sloppy, almost beggerish, business casual and punk.

We both looked at her and said "punk?" at the same time.

"Yes punk" she said. It was all the rage with the young teenagers in South Africa. Spiky hair. Lots of tattoos, heavy jewelry and unique clothing. The authorities will be looking for three middle aged adults. If we can blend in with the teenagers, we might have an advantage.

And I almost forgot, two Glocks with four spare clips of ammo each. This made us both sit up with wide eyes. She said "well don't you want to protect yourself? I sure do." We had to agree she was right.

Tom was out of food. He was still hungry so I shared some of my food with him. He needed the nourishment to heal.

The stress of the night, finding out that he was the cause of them running, the thought that he had a contagious disease and the accident itself showed on his face. He asked if he could take a nap. We got him situated back in the sleeping bag and he was soon asleep.

Mary and I moved a little down the hallway so we could talk and not disturb Tom.

CHAPTER 81

We decided that Mary would start exploring while I watched over Tom. As Mary walked away, the depth of our troubles began to sink in. We were in an underground catacomb, with no map or guide, a limited amount of food and water, no known exit (as we had just collapsed the way we got in), Tom has a broken leg with limited mobility, we can't go back to our apartment or jobs and we have a bunch of bad guys chasing us.

With all this going on, I decide I would spend the time in prayer while watching Tom sleep. I must have fallen asleep myself because I didn't hear Mary coming back. She was a little put off with me sleeping but covered it up well. Tom must have heard us talking because he woke up shortly after Mary's return.

She had been gone about ninety minutes and walked about 2 miles down the main hallway and some of the side hallways. She had found a small room which looked like it had once been a meeting room or sanctuary. She suggested that we move everything down there. It would be more defensible, it would get us out of the main hallway and it would also get us away from the tunnel that we used to get into the catacombs.

We both agreed with her and started working on how to move everything. Tom said he could use his crutches which would allow us to use the wheelchair as a means to carry our food, water and other supplies.

As we started our procession to The Sanctuary, as we would call our temporary home, I could see that Tom was still in a lot of pain. Even though he was showing the pain, he never once complained. He wasn't fast but he wouldn't stop and wouldn't let us put him in the wheelchair.

After about 45 minutes we came to The Sanctuary. It was just what we needed. The room was about 20x13 in size and had built in benches along the back and two sides. The front was plain except for two small cutouts in the wall about three feet long and two feet high. I could imagine an alter or podium placed between the two cutouts.

We began to set up home. We put the storage containers on the benches in the back. We considered using the benches on the side for sleeping but they were a little narrow. We were concerned that we might fall off. Before moving forward with this theory,

Tom volunteered to try sleeping on the benches. We told him that Mary and I were going to go out exploring together and that he should stay here. We gave him one of the Glocks and headed out.

Mary wanted to walk the main hallway to see where it went. From her research, she felt that the main hallway ran for about 10 miles. She thought that we were about two miles from one end and about eight from the other end. She also felt that the exit near the train station would be about four miles.

We needed to find a way out or a way to get fresh water so off we went.

We had walked about three miles when we saw some daylight. Mary signaled to me that we needed to stay quiet and up against the wall. As we crept forward, we were both excited and concerned that a small amount of light was coming into the hallway.

When we finally got to the source of the light, we found a steel door that was bolted on the other side. Not sure what was on the other side, we were careful to not make a lot of noise. Determining that opening this door was not going to be easy, we continued down the hallway.

Another mile down the hallway, we came to a door similar to the first one. Again it was locked from the other side so we continued on our search.

In the next mile, we found two more identical doors. We were starting to get frustrated and discouraged and we could see it in each other's faces.

Another mile or so, we found a possible escape route. Up near the top of the ceiling was a metal grate that looked like it might be an air duct. This made us realize that we hadn't been looking up during our exploration. Were there other grates that we missed? We decided to make sure we looked up on the way back.

The grate was too high for us to reach so Mary talked me into the old cheerleading routine. I became the base, allowing her to climb up on my shoulders. She was then tall enough to look for a latch or see if the grate could be opened. My shoulders began to hurt before she could find anything so we decided we would come back with the wheelchair and one of the tubs to stand on.

With renewed enthusiasm, we headed back. We noted that it took us fifty-seven minutes to walk back to The Sanctuary. We also noted four other grates identical to the one we had first found on the way back.

Hopefully, we would be able to open one of them.

CHAPTER 82

When we got back to The Sanctuary, Tom was awake. We updated him on our explorations, talking about the doors and the grates.

We decided to try all the grates first. As we gathered the tools that Mary had stashed, we found a pair of walkie-talkies. Mary was excited that she had remembered to pack them and started doing the happy dance. These would make exploring safer and if we could get out of the catacombs, communicating from the inside to outside safer.

We loaded Tom into the wheelchair after much debate. He wanted to be brave and use his crutches but Mary and I emphatically told him no. We would need his strength and his wits when we got to the grates and using his crutches would only wear him out. Besides we were in a hurry to get back there and weren't willing to go at crutches speed. After we had Tom in the wheelchair, we piled all the supplies in his lap and off we went.

We got back to the first grate in about 30 minutes. Our first thought on getting one of us high enough to work on the grate was for Mary to stand on my shoulder again. This only lasted for a few minutes. Our next thought was to have Mary stand on Tom's shoulders. Though he was stronger and probably could have held her for pretty long, with the cast and crutches he wasn't very stable.

Tom then thought of using the wheelchair. He sat in the chair and had Mary climb up on the handles used to push the wheelchair. This height was lower than standing on our shoulders but just high enough for Mary to work on the lock.

After thirty minutes of working on the lock, we gave up. We decided to try the next grate. Packing up our tools and supplies, we wheeled Tom down the hallway.

The second grate was just as stubborn. After spending another thirty minutes we gave up again.

The third grate was as stubborn as the first two and we were beginning to get discouraged. What if we couldn't get one of these grates to open? Would we be stuck in here for the rest of our days? Mary didn't seem as concerned as Tom and I, and I began to wonder if she had anything else up her sleeve.

We decided to give the fourth grate a try before heading back for some food and rest. Mary was up there doing her magic for about fifteen minutes and was about ready to give up when the lock clicked open. Tom and I started to cheer until Mary told us to keep quiet. We didn't know where the tunnel led and if someone could hear us on the other side.

With the grate open, it was time to go exploring. Mary looked at me and I realized that I was the chosen one to be the rat in the tunnel. Mary was claustrophobic enough that when we were together, I had to be the person to do the exploring in the small areas. I just prayed that there weren't any critters along the way.

I took one of the walkie-talkies and a flashlight and headed down the tunnel after a big kiss and hug from Tom. The tunnel was fairly clean except for the occasional spider web which creeped me out each time I crawled through one. Fortunately, I didn't see any of the spiders that made the webs.

Have you ever gone exploring down a tunnel or new path? If you have, you know that it seems like forever to get there because the anticipation heightens your expectations. I crawled for what seemed like an hour only to realize that it was about 10 minutes before I saw light at the end of the tunnel. I stopped and radioed back to Mary and Tom telling them that I was turning the volume on the radio way down and turning off my flashlight.

When I got to the end of the tunnel, I found another grate with another lock. I also found that it was dark on the other side though my clock said it should still be daylight. It appeared that I was in a large room though I couldn't tell how big because it was hard to judge the distance in the low light.

I radioed back my findings and told them I was going to see if I could get this lock open. After about five minutes and a few short prayers, the lock sprung open. I opened the grate slowly, trying to minimize the noise and was surprised that it moved freely and quietly.

I poked my head out to get a better look around. I found that I was about fifteen feet above the ground in what appeared to be a large warehouse. There was machinery parked throughout the warehouse, mostly of the road maintenance kind. I realized that if I got down to explore, I wouldn't be able to get back up again so I stayed in the tunnel.

I closed the grate and replaced the lock without engaging the locking mechanism and was starting to turn around when some lights flickered on at the far end.

Two men came through the door wearing uniforms of some kind. As they walked through the room, lights turned on automatically as if they were controlled by motion sensors. Not good. They continued to walk directly to where I was located so I moved back into the tunnel and lay flat. I knew that they wouldn't be able to see me from the ground but I still held my breath and didn't move. As they got closer, I could hear them talking.

They were arguing with each other. One was saying that he saw the motion sensors had shown movement while the other was saying that if there was movement the lights should have been on. They continued to argue as they did a search of the area below me and gratefully they didn't find anything.

I could hear them heading back so I slowly moved back to the grate to watch them leave. What I saw was a bunker full of military equipment. My heart sank as I realized that this tunnel wasn't going to be our way to safety.

I turned around and crawled back to the catacombs.

When I got back to Mary and Tom, I filled them in on all that I saw. Tom was disheartened but Mary was excited. This confirmed where we were in the catacombs. Her research had shown a large warehouse a quarter of a mile from the train station. Which meant that the next grate was the grate we needed to unlock.

We were all tired and hungry so we decided to head back to The Sanctuary for food and rest before tackling the next grate.

CHAPTER 83

Dinner was more protein bars, canned tuna and crackers. As hungry as we were, it tasted good. Tom wasn't as hungry today as he normally is which concerned me. He ate what was given to him and didn't ask for seconds. We skimped on the amount of water we drank, trying to ensure that we didn't run out.

We got Tom back in the sleeping bag and he was asleep pretty quickly. Mary and I took some of the clothes and laid them on the floor to try to keep some of the cold from seeping in. Mary was ready for bed but I wasn't.

Even though I was tired, I needed some time to myself to think. I told Mary I was going to go explore the Hallway the other direction towards the short side. I took one of the walkie-talkies and one of the Glocks and headed out.

As I walked up the Hallway, I reflected on the events of the last two days. How had Tom broken his leg and then gotten so far off the path? How had Rebecca fooled me into thinking she was one of the Few? Was there a second Rebecca or someone posing as Rebecca? How large of an organization were we being chased by that they could embed themselves into a hospital with that much ease and that quickly? Had they known about us before the accident? If so, why didn't they do something earlier?

With my mind wondering and me not paying attention, I almost missed the candy bar wrapper laying on the floor. It brought me back to reality in a hurry and had me focused on the here and now.

I picked up the wrapper to see if I could determine how long it had been there. The wrapper still looked new and none of the colors had faded. There weren't any bugs on or near the wrapper but that didn't really mean anything since I hadn't seen any bugs except for the few spiders in the air tunnel. I smelled the wrapper but couldn't smell any chocolate. Given the few facts I knew, my guess was the wrapper had been there for a while.

But how would a wrapper get into the catacombs without a person bringing it in? I started focusing on my surroundings and noticed a grate above me. Had the wrapper been blown in through the grate? Or were there others who had found a way in?

With no answers, I continued down the hallway much more alert with Glock in hand. Thirty more minutes of walking found me at the end of the hallway.

There was an elaborate arched doorway with beautifully carved wooden doors. My guess was the doors weighed thousands of pounds each. I was in awe of their beauty though there was a darkness about the carvings. In all my research, I hadn't seen anything like them. I stood and listened for about ten minutes to see if I could hear anything.

While standing there, I noticed that the dirt around the doorway seemed more trampled than what I had noticed in other parts of the Hallway. Was this a functioning door? Is this where the candy wrapper had come in through? What was on the other side?

Always the brave or stupid one, I'm not sure which, I checked to see if the doors would open. Much to my surprise, the massive doors open slowly and quietly. They revealed an ancient room with some of the most unique paintings I had ever seen. Upon entering, I also sensed a life force living in the room. One that was both dignified yet revolting. I needed to get out of the room and closed the door as quickly as possible. Once outside with the doors closed, I could still sense the life force and could also sense that the door helped keep it inside.

Standing there catching my breath I thought, so how did people get into this room? And then I saw this tiny passage leading off the Hallway. I would have missed it had I not been pasted to the wall. I thought about exploring the passageway but decided caution was the better part of valor. I could only be brave or stupid a limited number of times a day and I already had been there twice.

I headed back to the Sanctuary to catch Mary and Tom up on my findings. Along the way, I noticed a few footsteps heading down the Hallway but they stopped just after rounding the first corner. Had someone come down the Hallway far enough to not be seen? Another unanswered question.

When I got back, Mary and Tom were sleeping and I realized that I was exhausted. I crawled under the blanket with Mary and quickly fell asleep. Unfortunately, the night was filled with some unwelcome dreams.

CHAPTER 84

In the morning I caught Mary and Tom up on my findings from the previous day. They were excited to get exploring but I wanted to go more slowly. Neither of them had been in the room and I could still feel the negative life force.

I was also concerned about the foot traffic. I felt that if we needed to run or fight, Tom would be a liability on crutches. He was disappointed with my assessment but I was firm in my stand. Mary and I would go exploring and Tom would stay in The Sanctuary with a radio and one of the Glocks.

With a plan in place and our stomachs somewhat full from power bars, Mary and I headed out. This second time down the Hallway allowed me to be more observant of my surroundings. I pointed out two more grates to Mary and we found one additional door.

We stopped at this door because it was different than the others. It was recessed in a small alcove and appeared to be made of stone. Had we not been looking closely, we would have walked right past it. Wanting to get down to the passage, we decided to spend more time with the door on the way back. We made a mark in the dirt about ten yards down the Hallway to give us a visual when we were coming back but far enough away that if someone else saw our visual they wouldn't know why it was there.

When we got to the end of the Hallway, everything was eerily quiet. I slowly opened the door to the room to give Mary a look. Upon entering, we both felt the life force. I also noticed that it was stronger this time than last. Mary started walking towards the front of the room in an almost mechanical walk after only a few seconds. I grabbed her by her arm and I pulled her out of the room.

The look on Mary's face was scary. She was almost in a trance. Slowly she started to come out of it but it took a good five minutes for her to be totally back with me. We stood there for another five minutes before Mary felt that she was OK to move on. I'm not sure what was in the room but I wasn't going to let Mary back in.

I pointed out the features I had seen yesterday. Once Mary was up to speed, we headed down the hidden corridor. We kept our flashlights off even though it forced us to go slower. We didn't want to tip someone off who might be coming the other way.

The corridor was about fifty yards long. The walls were smooth the entire way and there weren't any noticeable walkways off of it. It had quite a few twists which forced us to go even slower every time we rounded one of the corners. At the end of the corridor was another door. This door was made of steel like the other ones we had seen in the Hallway though there were no handles or locks.

Mary and I were feeling around trying to decipher how it opened when we heard voices on the other side. We could hear them playing with a locking mechanism and both realized at the same time someone was opening the door. We started sprinting down the corridor hoping to stay ahead of whoever was coming.

Fortunately for us, we made the first bend in the corridor before the door fully opened. We continued our sprint past the weird room and up the Hallway to where I had seen the footsteps end last night. I pulled Mary over and we waited to see who was coming.

After what seemed like forever, two males dressed as monks in black robes came out of the corridor. They were deep in conversation and didn't notice two people spying on them. They walked up to the wooden doors and entered the room.

Once the door was closed, Mary and I looked at each other and took a big breath. We had found a way out though we weren't sure we wanted to use it. The monks' outfits looked like something out of a horror movie and neither one of us was convinced we wanted to go there.

We decided to wait to see if we could follow the monks back down the corridor and figure out how they opened the door. We checked in with Tom to give him a quick update and to let him know we would be longer than expected.

We waited close to an hour for them to come out. They started down the corridor in conversation which helped cover the minimal amount of noise Mary and I made following them. We got to the last bend in the corridor about the same time they got to the door. One of the monks opened a hidden box on the right side of the door and punched in a five digit code which caused the door to swing open into a small room. As the monks walked through, we could see that the room looked like a storage closet.

I asked Mary if she was able to pick up the numbers the monks entered. I had seen that the first number was a 1 and Mary agreed. She guessed that the second number was a 9 based on the monk's hand movements and I had seen the last number was a 7. So we guessed that the combination was 19xx7. That left a lot of choices but was a good start. With no answers, we headed back to The Sanctuary.

Both Mary and I had forgotten about the other door we found earlier until we saw our markings on the floor. We looked all around the door for some way to get it open. With our knowledge from the monks, we decided to start pushing on the wall on the right side of the door about shoulder high. On Mary's fifth or sixth push, a little door sprang open revealing another keypad.

I was going to touch the keypad when Mary grabbed my arm. She wanted to see if any of the keys had residual oils on them. If so, we would know what keys made up the combination. She reached down and picked up some of the fine dirt that lay on the floor. She then gently blew the dirt onto the keypad. Sure enough, five keys held some of the dirt. Those keys were 1, 3, 5, 7 and 9. If this door was controlled by the same monks and they weren't smart enough to use a different combination, then our combination to the two doors was either 19357 or 19537.

We talked about opening the door but decided to head back to Tom and work on a plan. We had a guess of what was on the other side of the door the monks went through but no idea what was on the other side of this door. Best to have a plan and all our guns before giving it a try.

CHAPTER 85

We got back to Tom and filled him in on our adventure. Mary and I had been talking the whole way back about what could be behind the stone door and where it could lead. We wanted to start there and suggested this to Tom.

Tom had also been thinking. His thoughts were that both doors would be risky. We didn't know what was behind the stone door and just a glimpse into what was behind the steel door the monks went through.

His thought was to first see if we could get into the grate that was next to the one we had opened yesterday. If we could get into the grate and through the tunnel, we may not have to face whatever was on the other side of the two doors. Mary and I had to agree with Tom that it might be best to spend half a day focused on the grate before opening Pandora's door.

With a plan in place and another power bar in our stomach, we loaded up Tom on the wheelchair along with our tools and headed down the Hallway. The walk to the grate seemed shorter today. Not sure why but maybe it was all the thoughts that kept running through my head.

When we got to the grate, we positioned the wheelchair below it with Tom sitting in it. Mary climbed up on Tom and then to the handlebars so she could reach the lock. Five minutes of yanking, pulling, pushing and swearing later the lock opened.

I was again voted as the best person to crawl through the tunnel and do the exploring. This tunnel was about the same length as the other tunnel and was also pretty clear of bugs. When I got to the other end, there was an identical lock and grate as before.

In looking through the grate, I saw a large tunnel stretching in each direction. When looking to my left, I saw a glow coming from down the large tunnel.

I started working on the lock when I heard this low rumble. I couldn't figure out what it was and it continued to get louder. Suddenly, the rumble turned into a roar and a large rush of wind followed by a train rumbling just below the grate. It scared the shit out of me. I had to sit there for a few minutes to calm down. I realized that this grate would get us out of the catacombs without really being seen.

I radioed back to Mary and Tom my findings and I could hear their excitement. I told them that I would work on getting the lock open before heading back their way.

This lock was a real pain in the ass. It took me almost 30 minutes to get it open. Along the way I had to answer three calls from Tom and Mary asking me where I was. Patience was not with those two.

While trying to get the lock open, two more trains came by. The noise and the wind were unsettling but knowing what was coming was soothing. Once I got the lock open, the grate opened easily. I waited for the next train to come by before poking my head out. The light I saw coming from my left looked like the station and it appeared that someone could get from the grate to the station in between trains without being noticed.

I closed the grate and headed back to Mary and Tom. Once back, Mary wanted to have a look also. We boosted her up into the tunnel and off she went. About 30 minutes later, she poked her head back out, satisfied that I had reported all that was to be known.

I had dreaded this success because it meant that one of us was going to have to go out in public. We ruled Tom out immediately. I volunteered but Mary said it should be her. If one of us was caught, the bad guys would rather have me. I couldn't argue with her logic though Tom was a little confused on this line of thinking. We didn't enlighten him.

Mary would take one of the walkie-talkies and one of the guns. I would lower her down to the tracks right after a train went by, pull the rope up and close the grate. She would run to the platform and hopefully get there before the next train came through. When she was ready to return, she would call us from the platform.

We decided that this first exploration would be at most one hour. Her job would be to do surveillance on the train platform and the surrounding area along with getting more water. I would stay in the tunnel down by the grate in case she got done early. We also decided to wait until around 5:00 pm when the station should be busiest.

At 4:45, Tom lifted us both up to the tunnel and off we went.

CHAPTER 86

EL and I were in position at the end of the tunnel. We thought of tying one end of the rope around the grate but realized that this could be seen from the outside. Instead, we tied the rope around EL's midsection and she would be the support for me to climb down and back up.

The train came by at 5:03 pm. As soon as it was out of sight, we opened the grate and I climbed down. I began my sprint down the tracks to the platform.

The platform was further away than I thought, as I continued my sprint down the tracks. As I neared the platform, I stayed as close to the wall as possible. I needed a way to get from the tracks to the platform before people on the platform noticed me. Just as I was thinking that I would need to leap up onto the platform, I saw a set of steps cut into the wall. I said a quick prayer of thanks, climbed the steps and found myself in a hidden alcove at the end of the platform. I stopped and said a second prayer. It had been four minutes from leaving EL to getting safely on the platform. I radioed back to EL that I had made it and how long it had taken.

I stayed hidden in the alcove until the next train arrived. Once it started discharging passengers, I tried to blend in with the crowd exiting the station. I didn't realized how much I missed the open sky until I stepped out of the station. The sunshine was radiant.

I started a reconnaissance of the area to determine the number of food establishments, what type of food and what type of person was buying from each establishment. I wanted to make sure that I blended in with the folks around me. I also was counting the different convenience and grocery stores. If I was going to be coming out of the tunnels regularly, I didn't want to frequent a store often enough that they would recognize me.

After walking three blocks in each direction, I had counted eleven fast food stores, three restaurants and one food truck. I also counted four convenience stores, two of which sold gas. I only saw one grocery store.

EL and I had decided that our most pressing need was water. This was something everyone needs daily but it is so hard to transport. We had calculated that if I could get two gallons of water it would last us two days. It was also the most water we figured I could carry and not look too suspicious.

I was mulling this dilemma over in my head when I passed a boutique selling purses and shoes. A large purse would let me hide quite a few water bottles and a satchel would let me hide most everything else I purchased. One hundred dollars later, I had a non-descript, boring new purse and a stylish but bland over the shoulder backpack/satchel combination bag.

My first stop was one of the gas stations. I bought two large bottles of water, two Pepsi's and a bag of chips. I put everything in the backpack except for the bag of chips which I opened and savored.

The next stop was McDonald's. They had started selling breakfast all day so I purchased six breakfast burritos. Easy to carry and pretty flexible. These went into my purse. I didn't want them squished by the water.

I stopped at a second convenience store and purchased a bottle of water and a Dr. Pepper, EL's favorite.

The final stop was the grocery store. Here I bought scissors, styling gel, a couple of tops, power bars, nuts and three more bottles of water. Once I got everything into my two bags, they were full and getting heavy.

I headed back to the train station. I needed to get there while there were still crowds. Upon entering the station, I noticed a few people just milling around who didn't seem to fit in. I quickly found two young girls engaged in conversation and pretended to be with them. I was able to slip down to the platform undetected.

When I was safely back in the alcove, I radioed EL. She was panicky. I hadn't realized it but I had been gone for ninety minutes, well over my estimated time.

She said the last train had gone by her about six minutes previous. I would need to wait about four more minutes before running back to the grate. Fortunately, the trains ran pretty much on time and soon I was sprinting back down the tracks. I saw the rope hanging down and EL's smiling face.

Climbing the rope was difficult with the two bags. I was struggling to get to the top when we heard the low rumble of the next train. Adrenaline kicked in and I was in the tunnel. We pulled the rope up and got the grate closed just before the train arrived. We were going to have to devise another way to get the food up the rope.

EL and I crawled back down the tunnel to connect with Tom.

He had waited patiently though you could see he was a little on edge. We headed back to The Sanctuary and I filled them in on my adventure. Once we got back, we celebrated with our breakfast burritos and soda. It was a nice celebration.

CHAPTER 87

We decided that I should go back out on the street the next day. With it being Friday, it would be the last chance to get into and out of the train station with larger crowds for a few days.

When I was outside the first day, I had seen nightclubs that catered to both the Goth and Punk lifestyles. I decided to try out some of the new clothes I had purchased the day before and go Punk. EL and I dug through the jewelry that I had in our survival kit and found a nose ring. We layered on a bunch of bracelets, added gel to the hair and transformed myself into someone that looked like they were in their early twenties.

Dressed and ready to go, we headed down the Hallway to the grate. Tom helped EL and I up to the tunnel and the two of us scurried like rats down the tunnel. We got the rope tied around EL, waited for the train to pass, lowered me down to the tracks and off I ran.

I made it to the Alcove without incident. When the train arrived, I blended into the crowds and headed for the doors. While walking through the station, I noticed a heavier presence of people milling around all of which looked dubious at best. Questions that started running through my head were, Why had the security detail been enlarged? Had they noticed me from earlier? Was I going to be able to get back to the tunnel without being noticed?

I didn't have any answers as I exited the station so I decided to keep to the script of getting food and water and then heading back.

I went the opposite direction than I had the previous day. I figured that I wouldn't run into anyone that might recognize me and I wouldn't end up in any of the stores I was in before.

I stopped in three stores and purchased a bottle of water, a Coke and something to eat. I figured that it would be less obvious if I only purchased enough for me.

I had filled up my bags and was heading back to the train station when I noticed more "watchers" arriving around the station. I didn't like what I saw so I turned around and found a coffee shop where I could sit and think.

As I sat there thoroughly enjoying my coffee, my eyes settled on a shop across the street. It specialized in Goth clothing. Then the idea hit me to get a complete change of clothes and present a different image than what they were looking for.

The girl working at the store thought I was her age and bought my story that I wanted to go to a different night club tonight and needed a change of clothes before arriving. She told me about her boyfriend who had tried to go into a Punk nightclub with his Goth clothes on and was beaten up for even trying. She was a dream to work with and helped me get all the right clothes. I'm sure she was going to get a nice commission off my purchase but even so, she went above and beyond.

After I was transformed in my clothes, she said I was going to have to change my make-up. I guess my expressions showed and she said for me to stay right where I was. A few minutes later, she showed up with her purse and make-up to finish the transformation. When she was done, I didn't recognize me.

On the way out, she pointed out some really sweet hats. I hadn't thought of it but a hat would help hide my face. With my new outfit and hugs from my new best friend, I headed out.

I was able to slip into the train station unnoticed. It seemed that the watchers knew what they were looking for and it was not a young girl dressed in Goth. Once in the Alcove, I radioed EL.

The run down the tracks, the climb up the rope and the getting back into the tunnel was easier this time. We had the rope up and the grate closed before the next train arrived. We scurried back down the tunnel to hook up with Tom.

When I popped out of the tunnel, Tom said "wow. What happened to you"? I must have given him a look of incomprehension, to which he said "you changed your clothes."

I told Tom and EL about my observations and my shopping adventure. Tom listened thoughtfully to the whole story before making any comments.

His military trained brain must have kicked in during the conversation because he could only see one possibility. The bad guys must be tapping into the public surveillance camera system and were using facial recognition. And if that was the case, our ability to get into and out of the train station was compromised. We had been walking for about 10 minutes when he made us stop and head back to the grate. He said we needed to get the locks back on the grates. He also said we needed to put a bunch of dirt on the locks and the grates so they didn't look used. As far as he was concerned, we could no longer use that route.

Grudgingly we headed back to secure the area. EL crawled down the tunnel with a container full of dirt and dusted the grate and lock. She secured the lock and headed back. While she was gone, I dusted down the grate on our side and had everything ready to lock up when EL returned.

We walked back to the Sanctuary in silence. Instead of enjoying the food I had purchased, we just ate it to be full.

CHAPTER 88

After dinner, we sat around talking about different ideas on what to do next. We decided a few things. First, we were going to try opening more of the grates to see where they took us. We needed a safe way to get out of the catacombs when it was time.

We also decided to see what was behind the 'brick' door with the hidden keypad. None of us were really motivated to begin a new adventure so we hunkered down for the evening.

Tom was in good spirits in the morning. The pain in his leg had subsided overnight and he was actually starting to put some pressure on it. He was amazed at how quickly it was healing. Mary and I just looked at each other and had our own opinions.

We loaded up Tom and our supplies on the wheelchair and headed to the 'brick' door. When we got there, our plan was for Tom to try the two different combinations with Mary and I each holding a Glock aimed at the door. Once the door opened, the two of us would use standard military protocol for entering the room.

With everyone in place, Tom entered 19357. Nothing happened. He tried entering it again with the same results. To ensure he didn't enter it wrong, he punched the numbers a third time. Nothing.

We all looked and gave Tom the nod to try 19537. Slowly he entered the combination and the door hissed open revealing a dark room.

Mary and I entered following our plan. I went right and she went left. Neither of us detected movement so we began to look around. Behind Mary was a light switch. When she clicked it on, all three of us just stood there with our mouths wide open not believing what we saw.

The room was a weapons storeroom. It had all the toys a terrorist, radical group or doomsday society would ever want. There were pistols, shotguns, machine guns, grenades, a few rocket launchers and one or two items I didn't immediately recognize.

Tom was the first to speak when he walked up to one of the items I didn't recognize. He touched it with a reverence I hadn't seen him use on anything other than me. When I asked what it was, he said it was a highly classified weapon that used sound waves to disable people. It had been under development when he was working in Washington DC and he hadn't realized that it had made it out of prototype. Someone was well financed and well connected.

We continued to explore the room and found shelves of canned food in the back along with two large barrels. Tom knew what these were also. His company had manufactured similar systems for the Saudi's. They were water containment systems.

The tubing leading into the barrels indicated that the water was coming from the outside. He also found levers and gauges which allowed the automatic filling of the barrels to maintain maximum capacity or to shut the system off from the outside. On the side of one of the barrels was a log written in a language Tom didn't recognize.

Mary and I instantly recognized it as an ancient Hebrew dialect. It was a checklist of when the system had been inspected to ensure everything was in working order. Someone had been coming every three months with the last inspection being one month ago. If they kept to their schedule, they wouldn't be back for another two months.

We had found our food and water supply for the time we needed to stay in the Catacombs but also realized that we needed to up our vigilance. Whoever was coming here were not nice people.

Our plan had been to continue on to the steel door the monks had gone through but with this discovery, we decided to put that off until Tom was more mobile.

We took some of the food supplies, ensuring not to take the top box and trying to keep the column heights relatively the same. That way if someone did come into the room, they would see the normal accumulation of dust on the stacks and they would all appear to be uniform. We also took one of the Glocks so each of us now had a weapon.

We headed back to The Sanctuary to store our bounty. It had been a fruitful morning.

CHAPTER 89

After lunch, we began the process of opening grates. We skipped the first four we came to because we had been unable to open them and the fifth grate went to the train station. We also chose to skip the sixth grate because it was too close to the train station.

Mary worked for thirty minutes on the seventh grate's lock with no success. I worked another 30 minutes on the next grate's lock again with no success. Mary worked on the ninth grate's lock without it opening. We were getting a little discouraged.

It was my turn on the tenth grate's lock. When I started to do my magic, I realized that it was unlocked. We all wondered if this was a mistake or were others entering the Catacombs. We had been so blindly moving down the Hallway that we hadn't been taking notice of our surrounds.

Tom's military instincts kicked in again and he made us all stand still, listen and look. What we noticed was one set of footsteps that led further down the Hallway without returning. This left the question of Who had come through the tunnel and where had they gone?

With no answers, we decided that I would crawl down the tunnel to see where it went. Did I tell you earlier that I don't really like tunnels and don't really like bugs?

As I got near the end of the tunnel, I noticed that it had been used more often than just once. Upon getting to the grate, I found the lock in place but unlocked. It appeared that the grate was about seven feet off the ground. It opened to the outside and I saw the sky for the first time in many days. In assessing my surroundings, this grate opened to the train switching station. There were about a dozen rail lines spread out in front of me with one locomotive moving cars around. I radioed back my findings to Mary and Tom and headed back without disturbing anything. If we were going to use this tunnel, it would have to be at night.

With our success, we decided to try one or two more grates. As we headed down the Hallway, it made a sharp bend to the left. Tom also kept a sharp eye on the footsteps to see if he could determine where they exited.

The lock on the first grate we came to after the bend proved to be as stubborn as most of the previous had been. After 30 minutes of trying, we decided to move on. Shortly after leaving this grate,

Tom spotted a few more of the footsteps.

As we approached the next grate, Tom made us slow down. He got out of the wheelchair and started walking down the Hallway without his crutches. What he saw was a series of footsteps coming and going from this grate. When Tom got down and inspected the footsteps, he determined that they were old. At least three to six months old. We felt a little safer but knew we might not be alone.

Mary got up to try the lock and found this one unlocked also. She hopped down and Tom lifted me up to go exploring down the tunnel. When I got to the grate at the other end, the lock had been relocked but it only took me a minute or two to pick the lock.

This grate opened into what appeared to be the back storage facility for a flour mill. Pallets of different brands of flour were stored all around the floor. There wasn't a lot of movement. I radioed Mary and Tom and suggested the Mary come my way. With it being Saturday, we might be able to do some exploring during the daylight.

The grate was hidden behind several tall pallets of flour so I was able to lower Mary to the floor with minimal risk of exposure. She headed out with one of the walkie-talkies and her Glock to see what she could find.

Twenty three minutes later, Mary was back. We locked back up and headed back to get the debriefing with Tom. She confirmed it was a functioning flour mill. There were three people working in one corner of the plant but other than those three, she couldn't find anyone. There were multiple doors throughout the building so it would be easy to get in and out with minimal observation.

Now with two escape routes, we felt better about being stuck in the Catacombs. We headed back to the Sanctuary for dinner and some rest. It had been a long day of exploring and tunnel crawling.

CHAPTER 90

With plenty of food and water, we decided to not risk going outside until Tom was mobile. Tom thought we would be stuck for almost six weeks but he was making a remarkable recovery. At the two week mark, he was walking without the crutches. At the three week mark, he cut the cast off and declared himself ready to travel. He wanted to see the sky again.

One thing Mary and I noticed as Tom healed was that he began to age. From the time I met him, he had always looked like he was in his thirties. In just these past three weeks, he began to look like someone in their mid-forties. I knew that he wouldn't be young forever but the sudden acceleration of his aging was surprising.

Mary and I talked and our theory was that the accelerated healing had to draw energy from somewhere. This energy was coming internally and the consequence was his aging. We didn't know if the aging would stop once the leg was healed.

Another contributing factor could be the added stress. Tom wasn't eating as much as he normally did and was sleeping twelve or more hours per day. The extra sleeping made sense to us but the lack of appetite didn't.

With nothing to do, Mary and I spent a lot of time in prayer. I talked with God about our situation, what He wanted us to do next, where we should go and who was after us. I didn't get a lot of clarity. Mary was also deep in prayer and when we compared notes, it was obvious she wasn't getting a lot of clarity either.

We also spent a lot of time planning our next moves. We thought of everything from returning to the United States, to getting to London, to heading to Israel and to splitting up and each of us going our own way.

Our final decision was that we needed to stay together. We also felt that with the sophistication of the people looking for us that we couldn't use trains or planes. This left us the option of moving by automobile and limited our choices to Africa.

We knew that Namibia, Botswana, Zimbabwe and Zambia all spoke English. We guessed that our pursuers also knew that and would expect us to head to one of these countries. We decided that we would pass through Namibia and head to Angola which predominantly speaks Portuguese. Mary and I could speak it well enough and Tom would just have to learn.

As the day to leave arrived, we started going through our list of items to take and also what to do with the stuff we weren't going to take. We each had a backpack, Mary had the purse she bought and I got the over the shoulder satchel. The first things to go with us were the Glocks, the money and all the clothes. We included the make-up to allow us to change our look and had room for two wigs. We wanted to take some of the tools but they were just too heavy though we settled on a pair of pliers, a screw driver and duct tape.

We also decided to raid the weapons store room. We picked up additional ammunition, a few hand grenades and a brick of C4. We also filled up our water bottles and grabbed some of the condensed food.

This still left a bunch of stuff to leave behind. We didn't want to just leave it all in The Sanctuary or in the ammunitions room so we decided to hide them in one of the tunnels. We loaded everything on the wheelchair and headed down the Hallway one last time.

We decided we were going to leave via the flour mill. This left the tunnel to the train switching station as the obvious place to leave our excess stuff. We put the two tubs into the tunnel and then I pushed them far enough down the tunnel so they couldn't be seen from the Hallway.

In our explorations of the Hallway over the past weeks, we had found a small side walkway about a quarter mile past the tunnel to the flour mill so we walked the wheelchair down to this hallway. We didn't want to leave it in the middle of the hallway where it could be easily found. We hadn't seen or heard anyone during our three week stay but we wanted to be cautious.

Once back to our escape tunnel, Tom lifted Mary and then me up. We lowered the rope down to Tom and with both Mary and me holding the rope, Tom was able to make it up to the tunnel. We secured the grate and lock before heading to the flour mill.

We had chosen Saturday evening to leave. We had been monitoring the activity in the flour mill over the past two weekends to understand when it was the least busy. Our initial thought was that Sunday would be the best time but we found that their first shift of the week started Sunday at 10:00 pm and there were too many people moving around for us to be comfortable.

Saturdays had been slow and fortunately this Saturday was no different. Tom would be the first out of the tunnel. Getting him to the head of the line was funny. The tunnel was small and he had to get from the back of the line to the front of the line. We tried all different ways until we settled on having him lay flat on the tunnel and Mary and me crawling back over top of him. The laughing broke the tension we were feeling.

We lowered Tom down and then the backpacks. Mary went next and then me. I had to climb back up one of the pallets of flour to get high enough to secure the lock. We decided not to lock the lock in case we needed to make a quick scramble back into the tunnel.

We were a motley crew heading out into the night for the first time in over three weeks.

CHAPTER 91

We came out on the west side of town and Mary said she had a car stashed on the east side of town. She recommended that we take a longer route to the car, one that kept us in neighborhoods and on side streets. She didn't want us going into any high population areas that might also have street cameras.

We made slow progress. Even though Tom was mostly recovered from the broken leg, he had lost a good bit of his strength and stamina. Every thirty or forty-five minutes we needed to stop for Tom to recover some.

Twice during the walk, we had to run. Once, a big dog came chasing after us, protecting his territory. The second time we saw flashing lights coming our way. We initially hid in the shrubbery but when the police slowed down as if they were looking for something, we ran through backyards until we were five or six blocks away.

By now it was close to 3:00 am, so it was unusual for three people to be walking through the neighborhood. We found a park with a bathroom and decided to hole up in the bathroom until closer to dawn when people would be out walking again. Tom was grateful for the respite and immediately fell asleep. With Tom asleep, Mary and I continued to talk through our plan.

At 6:53 am, we headed back out. We had seen walkers and joggers passing by so felt it was ok to be moving again. We decided to break up into two groups. We decided that two girls walking and talking and one guy walking by himself was probably the most optimal way to split up. We also felt that with Tom's fatigue that he should go first so if he needed to rest, we would see him. Each group took one of the walkie-talkies and we headed out.

Along the way, we stopped for breakfast at a fast food restaurant. We reached our destination by 9:30 am.

Another surprise was in store for Tom and me. We ended up in a storage facility where Mary had rented two bays. The first bay had three beautiful, fast motorcycles. These the kind of motorcycles that would scream down the road leaving everything in their dust. The other bay had an older, nondescript car with tinted windows.

We all wanted to take the motorcycles but realized these would mark us as a threesome which is what the bad guys were looking for. Also, even though they would outrun anything chasing us, we couldn't outrun a helicopter.

Mary also had the storage facility fairly well stocked with food, water, two more Glocks and plenty of ammunition. This now left us with five Glocks and a lot of ammunition. She also had two phones and an iPad. Finally, she had passports for all three of us from the United Kingdom, South Africa, France and Egypt. Her theory was, you never know where you need to be from.

Neither Mary nor I had slept for about twenty four hours and needed rest. We made beds on the floor of the storage facility with plans to leave just after sunset.

Before heading out, Mary fired up the iPad and went to the City database. She wanted to understand where all the street cameras were so that we could navigate around them. She then mapped out the location of all street facing ATMs because they all have cameras to record the transaction. Overlaying the two provided us with a twisting route that would also allow us to leave the city without being recorded.

CHAPTER 92

We twisted and turned our way through the city and believed we avoided all the traffic cameras. We put Tom in the backseat and had him lying flat so if we did pass an unexpected camera, his image wouldn't be reflected through the window. I was made up to look like a young teenage girl and Mary was made up to look like my mother. We were just a mother and her daughter out for a ride.

After leaving the city, we took the highway towards Nambia. We did our best to stay near other cars as we traveled north but found that around 1:00 am the traffic became almost nonexistent. Feeling that we might be drawing attention to ourselves, we pulled over into a side road and hid the car in some foliage. Tom had been dozing off and on so he volunteered to be our lookout while Mary and I got some rest. Mary and Tom exchanged places and we did the best we could to get some shuteye.

With sunrise, traffic on the road began to pick up. We waited until about 8:00 am before joining the flow of vehicles moving up and down the highway. While we were waiting, Mary and I changed clothes and redid our makeup to resemble the pictures that were on our passports.

About five miles from the border is a scenic overlook that gives the observer a wonderful view of the valley. Tom decided to pull into the overlook for us to stretch and use the restroom. After using the restrooms, we stopped to take a ten minute break and enjoy the view. What we saw was a long line of vehicles waiting to get through the border crossing. One of the other people who had stopped overheard us talking and volunteered that he went up to Nambia every week for work and for the last three weeks, there had been long lines at the border crossing. They were taking their time in checking everyone's passport and asking their reason for leaving the country. Instead of what used to be a thirty second stop, he now had to endure a thirty minute wait. He said he now stopped at the overlook just to use the public restrooms.

The three of us knew why there was extra security at the border. We were going to stick out like a sore thumb so another plan was needed. Mary pulled out the iPad and started searching for other roads leading north. About five miles west and twelve miles east were secondary crossings. We felt that these would also be covered fairly well since they were easy alternate, backup routes.

About thirty five miles west, Mary found what looked like a tertiary crossing. There were no towns on either side of the border and it looked like it was mainly used by locals. We talked about the pros and cons of using this route. The pros were that it was most likely not manned, it was out in the middle of nowhere and it should allow us to pass over into Nambia without having to use our passports. The cons were that it was out in the middle of nowhere and could be watched by a single person some distance from the crossing and our car was not really made for an off-road drive.

Knowing that we couldn't continue on the path we were currently taking, we decided to head to the small village of Millvale which was about 9 miles south of the tertiary border crossing. We had to double back and then do some driving on what only resembled a road but made it to Millvale around 1:00 pm. It was a sleepy little place and we were instantly the talk of the town. We pulled over in front of the café and headed in for lunch.

We quickly found out that Afrikaner was the local language which required me to do all of the talking. I shared that we had been out for a drive and got turned around somehow. Blonde jokes are common around the world so I used that to my advantage. I shared how my sister and I insisted my husband follow our instructions even though he thought we should be going the other direction. When we became hopelessly lost, we finally admitted we were wrong and he was able to get us to here. Giving him a big kiss, I sealed the story.

By the time I was done, everyone was laughing at us and feeling sorry for Tom. They all knew how it was to be newly in love and wanting to please their mate. As we ate lunch, I asked them for directions.

They didn't think we should go back the way we came because they weren't sure we wouldn't get lost again. One of the locals recommended that we head over into Nambia where the road was better maintained and then circle back home. Another said that our car wouldn't make it to the border crossing because the latest rains had made it almost impassable.

After ideas from most of the others had been voiced, the older gentleman that had been sitting quietly in the corner spoke. When he spoke, the room became quiet. I mentally noted that we had found the town elder. He recommended that we load our car into the back of one of their trucks and they would drive us over the rough roads into Nambia. The idea immediately got the approval of all involved and the discussion moved to which truck would be big enough.

As we headed out, the older gentleman asked to speak with me. Quietly, he said he had seen a vision last night that he should help God's children. When we showed up, he knew we were the children who needed the town's help. He said that we would be safe for two days but peril was ahead. A tear came to my eye as he kissed my hand and said a simple prayer. He then discreetly gave me a small piece of paper which I put in one of my pockets.

We left the café to assist in the loading of the car. The elder suggested that the car be covered to keep it from "getting too dusty". Finally, he gave each of us a local jacket and hat to wear so that we would blend in. As we all loaded into the truck, I had to run over and give him one final hug. As we drove the nine bumpy and treacherous miles into Nambia, I reflected on how when God had a plan, He could use anyone to further that plan.

CHAPTER 93

We drove in the truck until we reached a spot a few miles north of the border. The driver said this is where he was instructed to drop us off by the elder. We unloaded the car, thanked the driver and watched him head home via a different road. He had instructed us to continue on the road for a while until we came to the next village.

As we started driving, Mary wanted to know what the elder said at the end. I said he just wanted to wish us good luck. Mary started pushing for a better answer until I gave her that look that said "later when we are alone".

Her prodding reminded me of the piece of paper the elder gave me so I delicately pulled it out of my pocket. On it was scribbled a name and an address. Mary pulled out her iPad and the address was two towns north and one town west of where we were. With no better place to go, we headed north.

We arrived into the dusty little village just before dusk. When we asked for directions, we were directed to a small house, more of a hut, near the center of town. As we pulled up to the house, another older man came out of the house. He looked a lot like the elder from Millvale and we would find out that they were cousins. I showed our new elder the note and he asked us in. Before coming in though, he wanted us to move the car into a small shed behind the house.

Upon entering the house, we realized that his wife had been cooking all day preparing a feast. After introductions, we realized that the elder's name roughly translated into Tomas and we all got a good laugh out of having two men both with the same name.

They fed us a simple but filling dinner. I'm not sure I know what I ate, nor do I really want to know, but it was good. After dinner, Tom looked exhausted so we talked him into going out to the car and getting some good sleep in the back seat. It was obvious that we were going to be sleeping in a corner of the house on the floor and though back seats aren't that comfortable they are more comfortable than the floor.

After Tom had been away for some time, Tomas shared that last night he had seen a vision. In his vision, guests would be sent to him by his cousin and that he should be a gracious host. He shared that vision with his wife who had then started cooking a dish which is a family tradition and is only cooked for special occasions. We thanked his wife many times throughout the evening for the wonderful food and hospitality.

The four of us talked for a few hours with me translating for Mary. Tomas shared about the history of his people and his village. He shared stories about his youth when he and his cousin used to meet at the annual games held between villages. And he shared stories of his family and the trials they had gone through over the years because of the civil wars. Both of his sons had been killed and his daughter lived in disgrace because she had been raped. We offered to pray for and bless his daughter if he wanted.

Mary and I were fading and ready for bed. Tomas and his wife made room for us on the floor next to the hearth. They then retired to the other side of the room behind a small tapestry to their bed. Mary and I just marveled at the day and each knew it was the hand of God that was directing us.

Before closing our eyes, I shared with Mary what the elder from Millvale told me as I was leaving. Each of the cousins had seen a vision designed to help us.

Tomas and his wife were up and moving long before any of us woke up. I marveled at how they moved so silently through the house. After being awake and receiving a small meal, Tomas asked if our offer to bless his daughter still stood to which we said yes.

He asked if we would follow him and we headed to the center of the village. As we came closer, we realized that the entire village had been assembled. Standing in the center of the crowd, in the center of the village stood a simple but beautiful young woman. Tomas explained that this was his daughter and our blessing in front of the village would purify her of her sins. Tears immediately came to my eyes and I could see them coming to Mary's eyes.

Once to his daughter, Tomas and his wife stepped back into the crowd. Tom and Mary also stepped back leaving me and his daughter. Totally unprepared, I did the one thing I knew how to do the best — pray. I held Tomas' daughter's hands and we sat down with our legs crossed. I began to pray out loud and silently, losing track of time. After what seemed like just minutes but was closer to two hours, I opened my eyes. Not a person had moved in the time and tears were freely flowing down the daughter's cheeks. Filled with the Holy Spirit, I said "in the name of Jesus Christ, your sins are forgiven". She stared at me for a long time and finally said

"Amen". And with that simple word, the village exploded into joyous approval. Tomas' faith had restored his daughter and would allow his lineage to continue through his daughter. A great party ensued and we stayed in the village for another night.

CHAPTER 94

As we were leaving the village the next day, Tomas gave me a small piece of paper with just a name and address. It was another cousin near the border of Angola that would provide a place to stop. Mary pulled out the iPad to get us going in the right direction and we followed her lead throughout the day. We didn't make quick progress and ended up spending the night in the car. The following day, we arrived in the village in mid-afternoon.

Asking for directions, we ended up in at a similar house again near the center of the village. After our first inquiry, one of the local villagers ran ahead and announced our coming. The elder wasn't too happy to see us even with the note from Tomas. He shared that people had been through the village two days earlier looking for us. He recommended that we not stay in the village. With another note and directions, we headed out. Had this been the trouble that the elder in Millvale had talked about? We would have been here two days previous if we hadn't prayed over Tomas' daughter and then gotten lost.

The directions led us back into Nambia and close to one of the major towns. After looking at where we were headed, we chose to go the other way. As night approached, we could tell we were approaching Angola. The road led us across an unmanned border crossing. We traveled on for another hour or so because we didn't want to stop close to the border. We saw a small town in the distance but decided not to head there in the dark. We found cover, ate out of the trunk and slept in the car.

Now that we reached Angola, we needed to decide where to hide. The obvious choice was the capital city of Luanda with a population of around 2.5 million. It should be easy to get lost there. But if it was the obvious choice for us, it would also be the obvious place to post watchers.

Our next choices were Huambo and Cabinda who each had a population of over 325,000. Cabinda was on the other side of the country and would take us too long to get there. We kept Huambo as a possibility.

Our final cities under consideration were Benguela, Namibe Lobito and Luena. We finally settled on Lobito. Before independence from Portugal, Lobito was one of the busiest ports in Angola. After independence and the civil war, it has begun to thrive again as a commercial shipping hub. We felt that with this history of trade, we would have the opportunity to blend in better. It might also offer us a way to exit Africa undetected.

Our trip through the center of Angola and then west to the coast was slow. We decided to stay away from the major cities and used secondary roads whenever possible. We stopped and ate at the local cafes, always taking time to talk to the locals. This gave us the opportunity to see if there was anyone unusual passing through other than us. It also gave us the opportunity to tell false stories of who we were so if others came asking about us, the locals would be less likely to talk.

Early in our trip, we had the opportunity to trade our car for a more practical but less comfortable off-road vehicle. We were taken advantage of but that was ok because we now blended in better. It did make it more difficult to sleep in the car which we did most nights.

CHAPTER 95

It was customary for the husbands to find housing so when we got to Lobito, we sent Tom off to find us a place to live. He looked the part of someone moving in from a small village. He hadn't shaved since his accident. All the time in the sun had given him a pretty good tan. The clothing we were wearing was appropriate along with looking and being well used. He didn't speak Portuguese but with the right passport and his Afrikaner dialect, he passed for a local.

While Tom was looking for a place to stay, Mary and I went shopping for traditional African head wraps. The one we were wearing marked us as being from outside the city and we needed to blend in. We also needed to purchase some local dresses and update our make-up. By the time we were supposed to meet back up with Tom, we looked like local women.

Tom's journey was a little more difficult. The first few places that Tom went to obviously didn't want to rent to him because he wasn't local. His inability to speak Portuguese was a deterrent. Frustrated, he stopped to have a cup of coffee. Listening to the conversations going on around him, he heard two men speaking English. Tuning in to their conversations, he realized that they were watchers looking for the three of us.

When they got up to leave, Tom finished his coffee and decided to follow them. Staying well back and out of site, he watched them go into a small office. The office had two laptops that they were supposed to be monitoring but fortunately, they were not. He and the girls would need to come back to investigate later that night.

This encounter changed where he went looking for housing. He would need to search outside the middle class area. Continuing to walk the streets, he was unsuccessful in finding a place before needing to head back to meet with us.

His discouragement showed on his face when we saw him. He filled us in on his day and his discovery made us all very hesitant. We talked about staying in Lobito or heading back out. Ultimately, we knew that as long as we were in Africa, we would run into watchers.

As we walked back to our car, Mary spotted a small sign in the window of one of the shops. She asked Tom and me to go window shopping while she went inside the store. We casually walked across the street where we could observe her through the reflection in the windows.

After a few minutes of discussion, a small child came out of the store and headed our way. She asked us to follow her and with a nod from Mary we headed down the street and around to the back of the store. We came into a small, warm home with two other small children. Mary and the storekeeper appeared shortly afterwards.

Mary began to explain. During the civil wars that had occurred throughout Africa, the equivalent of an Underground Railroad formed for smuggling people around, into and out of Africa. The storekeeper had been part of the Underground Railroad and still did some smuggling though he considered it trading. Mary had convinced him to listen to our story as we solicited his help.

We spent the rest of the afternoon with the storekeeper telling a made up story of drugs and prostitution. Tom had fallen in love with EL while buying her services. He had convinced the two of us to run away with him. All three of us were now on the run and needed to get to a better place.

He bought into the story and agreed to help us. We would stay with him that night while he went out to make inquiries. After the store closed and we had dinner with him, he showed us to a small room in the back of the store where we would stay for the evening.

The storekeeper came back some hours later. One of the people who he had worked with before had a ship leaving for Australia in the morning where we could get passage. The ship's owner wanted far more money than we had available so we proposed the following: half of the cash we had on us plus the key to the safe deposit box back in South Africa. It contained about twice what the asking price was. The storekeeper came back a few hours later with a deal. We would need to leave immediately to get to the ship.

Scurrying through the night, moving from shadow to shadow, we approached the docks. The storekeeper introduced us to the ship owner. We provided the cash and the key and were taken to the ship. We gave the keys to the car to the shopkeeper for his troubles. We weren't going to be needing it again.

Our quarters on the ship where cramped for the three of us but that was a small price to pay for getting safely out of Africa. The trip to the western coast of Australia was uneventful.

CHAPTER 96

Our first purchase after getting off the ship was a pre-paid mobile phone. Mary called one of her guy friends who lived in Sydney. After a short conversation, the two of them hung up. Her friend had a few friends who lived nearby and he was going to make a few calls on our behalf. Since we had some time, we decided to stop by one of the local cafes and get some food.

Mary's friend called back while we were enjoying our post meal cup of coffee. One of his friends was willing to let us stay with him for a few days. We were given the address and told to go to the guest house off the back of the property. Mary's friend also said that he had some time off coming his way so he was going to catch a plane and would be able to join us tomorrow. Mary was excited.

We picked up some provisions and headed to the guest house. It had one bedroom along with a pull out couch, a small kitchen area and one bathroom. We all eyed the shower with envy and playing rock, paper, scissors to see who would go first. Mary won the right to be first in the shower. Tom and I put the groceries away and checked out our new surroundings.

When Mary was done, Tom and I jumped into the shower. It was heavenly. I trimmed Tom's beard down to something more manageable, keeping enough to hide his features. After the trimming, I saw that Tom had aged even more during the ship ride. He now looked like he was in his mid to late fifties.

After the showers, the three of us sat on the back porch. Mary's friend had recommended that we stay close to the house until he got there and could introduce us to some of the locals. They didn't take too kindly to strangers.

It had been a long time since we could safely sit and talk. I asked Tom how his leg was doing. He said that it stopped hurting during the ship ride and he felt it was healed. He commented on how he was a lot more tired lately. Asking if it was ok to take a nap, we sent him in to try the bed.

After a while, I went and checked on him and he was sleeping. When I came back out, I asked Mary if she noticed anything different about Tom. She said that he looked a lot older than he had before the accident. We didn't fully understand what was happening to him but knew that changes were happening fast. We speculated that the accident triggered something inside him and that his agelessness was maybe coming to an end. I ached inside.

That evening, I brought up the subject of Tom looking older. He agreed that he was looking older and that some of his energy was no longer there. He wasn't sure what was happening. We speculated with him that whatever had kept him young for so many years could be wearing off. I held his hand and he held mine each knowing that the truth had been spoken.

Mary gave us the bedroom that evening and for the first time in a long time, we had a sleepless, romantic night.

CHAPTER 97

Mary's friend Evan arrived the next day. You could tell that Evan was head over heels for Mary because sparks kept flying across the room between them. It made me smile.

Evan took us to one of the local pubs for dinner. The food was simple but was the best we had had in a long time. We savored every bite. Tom even got extra bread so he could soak up the gravy on his plate and mine.

After a few beers, Evan asked the question we knew was coming – "What brings you here?"

We had worked on an answer the night before. We explained how we had been living in South Africa. Tom had a job at a manufacturing company that shipped product around the world. He had gone into work one Sunday to catch up on paperwork and stumbled into what we found out was a large smuggling operation being run by the Chief Financial Officer. The CFO was working in the black diamond trade and would conceal diamonds in some of the shipments.

When Tom confronted the CFO some really bad people came after him. Tom went to the police only to find that one of the detectives was working with them and nearly got Tom killed. Not knowing who to trust, we used one of Tom's owner's connections to get on a ship heading anywhere. That anywhere brought us here.

We needed to start a new life, under new names in a new country.

Evan bought into the story. He continued to ask us questions some of which we answered and some of which we couldn't answer. By the end of the night, his questions had changed from wanting to learn more about why we were here to how he could help us moving forward. He said he didn't have a lot of connections but would help however he could. We all agreed to begin working on a plan the next day when we could think a little more clearly.

We headed back to the bungalow and this time Mary and Evan got the bedroom. From their looks the next morning it had been a sleepless, romantic night.

CHAPTER 98

We sat out on the porch of the bungalow and planned our next moves. Evan knew a person who owned a resort about 50 miles outside of Perth. He made some calls and by the end of the day had secured us each a job at the resort. The pay was terrible but its remoteness offered us the opportunity to hide for a while.

Mary decided to fly back to Sydney with Evan for a few days leaving Tom and I alone. We stocked up at the grocery store before they left so we wouldn't have to go anywhere. There was a peacefulness about the place which we hadn't experienced in quite a few years.

Tom and I talked more about his getting old. He had been young for so long and the aging had come on so fast that he was genuinely worried. He was more worried about me than he was about himself. His biggest question was "Why aren't you and Mary aging also?" I didn't have an answer for him. Well I had an answer but I couldn't really share it with him.

We talked about what his wishes were when he passed away and we each knew the obvious though neither of us would say it.

Mary was back midweek with new passports and identification that showed us as citizens of Australia. She also had a stack of cash from somewhere. I had to marvel at how she had stuff stored around the globe.

Before Evan left, he had purchased a vehicle for us to drive. We had also gone clothes shopping so we would blend in better. Mary had paid him back for everything while in Sydney and we looked like locals again.

Our cover story this time was a father and his two daughters. Our mother had recently passed away and the daughters had convinced their dad to follow one of his childhood dreams of living near by the beach, getting up each day watching the sun rise over the water. Since we were going to be on the west coast, we wouldn't see the sunrise over the water but we would see the sunset every night. It was close enough for the storyline.

The drive to Perth was uneventful. Some nights we would stop in a town and get a room. Other nights we would drive until we got tired and then pull over and sleep in the car. We made it to the resort on Sunday afternoon and were greeted warmly by Evan's friend. He got us set up with our new jobs which would start on

Wednesday leaving us two days to get acquainted with the area.

He made a call to a friend of his who had a small property a few miles away. He was able to secure us the rental of another small bungalow for which we were most grateful. With a place to stay and two days of freedom, we explored the small town that supported the resort. On Tuesday, we found a small café hidden away at the end of a small alley that served the most wonderful, tasteful, and mouthwatering food we had experienced since Blue Moon West. Over the coming months, we would eat there at least once a week.

CHAPTER 99

We started our new jobs on Wednesday. The owner wanted Mary and me to work in a customer facing job like registration or waitressing or bartending but we told him we preferred to stay behind the scenes. We had been pretty popular back in Sydney and were trying to get away from that scene for a while. I ended up cleaning rooms while Mary ended up in the kitchen.

The owner was struggling with where to use Tom until we told him that Tom was both a mechanical and electrical engineer. The owner asked Tom if he was able to fix things and when Tom said usually, the owner gave him a long list of things that were broken. The two of them spent about an hour prioritizing the list marrying the owner's needs with Tom's skills.

After the first week, Tom had fixed the two most critical items and only had to drive into Perth three times. When the backup generator fired up the following Monday, the owner invited us to dinner with him the following day with anything we wanted on the house. We were told the bisque was to die for so we each had a bowl. We weren't lied to. Each of our dinners were top notch. And there was a surprise dessert – an orange cheesecake.

The owner was taken by surprise by the cheesecake having never had that on the menu before. The three of us weren't surprised. When we had all cleaned our plates of the cheesecake, Mary volunteered that she had talked the cook into allowing her to make it. It was her favorite dessert to bake, something she had made twice before for us.

The next day, the chef promoted Mary to pastry chef, a position they had never had before. Over the coming months, Mary would make some spectacular concoctions that started to create a buzz with the guests. Mary had found her calling and could be world renowned if she wanted.

We greatly enjoyed our time at the resort. The work was hard but that was OK. We had each other and there weren't any bad guys around.

Each week, we noticed that Tom was continuing to age. It was almost like he aged a year every week. This was a constant item of discussion and even though Mary and I could guess at the reason we couldn't share our thoughts with Tom. This broke my heart.

Three months into being at the resort, Tom collapsed at work. The owner wanted to rush him to a hospital in Perth but we were able to talk him out of it. We chalked it up to not eating right or not drinking enough water. The owner told him to take some time off which Tom agreed to.

That evening, I had a vision. God shared that Tom's time was quickly coming to an end. He showed me a motorhome in the middle of nowhere. Mary and I talked about the vision while traveling to and from work that day and came to the conclusion that we should be leaving the resort and doing some much needed sightseeing.

We talked about my vision with Tom. We felt that God was telling us that it was time for us to leave the resort. We also felt that if Tom had another incident while at the resort, the owner would insist on him going to Perth and we couldn't afford for that to happen. Tom showing up in the hospital would only bring the bad guys coming real quick.

Over the next week, we started looking for RVs to buy and places to visit that were out of the way. By the end of the second week, we acquired an older RV, had talked with the owner of the resort telling him that Tom needed a short vacation and that we hoped to be back his way in a few weeks. The owner was disappointed that we were leaving. And the guests were going to miss Mary's specialties. The one shining light was that Tom had made it through the list of broken mechanical items.

With goodbyes said and tears in our eyes, we left the resort for the last time.

It would be two weeks later when I would receive my last vision regarding Tom.

Epilogue

CHAPTER 100

Tom. Our Father shared with me that today will be your last day here on Earth. He will be calling you home before the sun rises again. I know you can hear me. I just know it.

I have asked our Father if I can share our story with you. It is a story that has never been told to anyone on Earth. It is only known to Mary and me. He has agreed.

I don't know how much you have guessed or surmised over the years. A lot of the stories I told over the years were meant as stories but each had a bit of truth in them.

CHAPTER 101

Let me begin at the beginning. Which is the logical place to start wouldn't you agree.

I can see you giving me that look of compassion, love, sympathy and angst that you always gave me when I wanted to tell you a story. Thanks for listening through the years.

My real name is Elizabeth. Mary is my twin sister. I am the older of the two.

Our parents are Adam and Eve. We were born to them while they lived in the Garden of Eden. We were a loving family until they ate the apple from the Tree of Life. God foresaw this and unbeknownst to the serpent, the apple also caused my parents to forget major portions of their past. They didn't recognize us after eating the apple so there is no written record of us once they were banished.

God had a plan for us and allowed us to stay and thrive in the Garden. As we matured into adulthood, God appeared one day and shared his plan. It was simple. We would each bear one of His sons. He said that Mary must remain a virgin until the appointed time for her to bear His first son. I was to bear His second son.

We have lived in and out of the Garden since the creation of time, being able to view history. In the year AD 2, God said it was time for us to leave for a while. He said that I would bear a child that would herald the coming of His first son and I was to name him John. He placed me where He wanted me to be with the father of John.

Mary was placed such that she would draw the attention of Joseph. As the Bible tells the story, an Angel came to Mary and told her that she would have a son. That same Angel visited and told Joseph to not be afraid as his son was conceived by the Holy Spirit.

I am here to tell you that the stories of Jesus in the Bible are true. Mary and I were there and have acted as scribe and memory to the authors.

CHAPTER 102

In the year AD 1991, God came to us again in the Garden. He said it is time for His second son to be born. The world had waited long enough.

He shared that a boy was born that year who would carry the seed of His son. We were instructed to go into the world again and find him. He shared we would know the man by his blood. Upon tasting his blood, we would know the strength of his seed. We were to choose wisely.

He also shared that it would be me to carry this child. He said Mary and I must work as a pair to identify the proper seed. He would provide visions and guidance but His son had to come via free choice and free will.

Thus we walked back into the world.

CHAPTER 103

I came to the University with a sense that I would find you there. I'm not sure what I was looking for. Mary and I were sure you would be an important person, either famous, a sports star, rich or gorgeous. I wasn't looking for you, though I have come to know that you are all of them and more.

Had you not been persistent in your pursuit of me, I would have missed you. I know in my heart that God influenced your pursuit of me and helped to keep you focused. The cutting of your finger that Thursday night so long ago was a blessing. How you could cut your finger on a piece of paper and then bleed so much, is beyond me. I guess God didn't want me to miss my one chance.

When I woke up from "kissing it to make it better", I saw the depth of your love in your eyes. As Jesus said in *God's Blue Book*, "the eyes are the doorway to the soul", and I truly saw you in that moment.

You scared the heck out of me!

Mary and I talked a lot after that first "kiss". We did a lot of scheming so I would win you over but in the end it was you who won me over.

I have a confession to make. Do you remember our discussions about having children and your adamancy of not having any? I remember the vision you painted about your abusive dad and your insistence of not having children. I remember how scared I was when you said you had a vasectomy done. How was I going to have your child?

That night, God came to me with my favorite line from the Bible – "Oh ye of little faith!" He said He would give me the power to heal you but there could be long term consequences. He said I could have the seed but must carry it until your death. Only after your death would I become pregnant. I have cried many tears over the years knowing I carry your seed but was not allowed to share that with you. You would have been an awesome dad.

CHAPTER 104

Do you remember that first night we made love? It is seared in my memory. I remember every minute and it was then that I realized I had fallen in love with you. My love, my human desire to spend forever with you caused me to create the long term consequences.

Instead of just healing the vasectomy, I healed all of you. I am sorry for the deception over the years.

All humans are born with defects. God shared with me that I had the power to perform a miracle, to heal your vasectomy. He also warned me to use caution. I didn't understand.

When we were making love, the healing flowed from me to you. I knew when your vasectomy was corrected but I couldn't stop. I let the healing flow until it consumed all of you. Even then, I couldn't stop. It was my inability to stop that pushed you to nearly passing out. I still laugh to myself at your reaction. A typical male response of not knowing what happened, saying this never happened before, apologizing profusely and then sulking.

Do you remember the second time we made love that evening? I was finally able to get you back into the mood and the second time was as good as the first. In all honesty, the 100th time was as good as the first, the 1000th time was as good as the first and the last time was as good as the first. Oh how I will miss you, miss your touch and miss your intimacy.

Chapter Last

Tom my love. We have come to the end of our love story. I have had many lovers but only one love. I am told that when we go into eternity, very strong emotions will follow us. I know that when I pass away, your memory will go with me. If two people possess a strong enough love for each other on Earth, they will reunite in Heaven. My prayer is that I get to spend eternity with you.

Goodbye my love!

ABOUT THE AUTHOR

Born in Pittsburgh, PA, I began moving around the United States after college first with the US Air Force and then following work opportunities. The Air Force introduced me to my wife and she has joined me on this adventure call life for 39 years.

Writing was never something I thought I would do well. But through many years of writing for work and through the grace of God, I have begun to enjoy putting words on paper.

I hope you have enjoyed this novel.

Ars longa, vita brevis.

www.facebook.com/ThePerfectKissByDennis

www.ingramcontent.com/pod-product-compliance
Lightning Source LLC
Chambersburg PA
CBHW020619180626
46810CB00007B/2849